A Game of Love

By Barbara Baldwin

Digital ISBNs
EPUB 978-1-77299-903-7
Kindle 978-1-77299-904-4
WEB 978-1-77299-905-1
Amazon Print ISBN 978-1-77299-906-8

A quality publisher of genre fiction.

Airdrie Alberta

Dedication

To my sister Linda,
who traipsed all over Boston with me in the cold and rain,
listening to me mumble about plot and characters.

Chapter 1

Megan tilted her head back as far as she could, and still the chimneys of the three story mansion were hidden from view. It stood separate and majestic among the brick row houses in the heart of Beacon Hill. More than two hundred years ago, it had been the only house at the very edge of Boston by the Charles River, home to a tea merchant during the Revolutionary War.

Stacy, her best friend since grade school, actually lived here now. When they were young they had called it the *Castle* and had often pretended a prince would ride up on his white horse and carry them away. Even now when she had outgrown childhood fantasies, Megan felt the house held secrets lost to time.

The wrap-around porch and tall front columns were painted a dark cinnamon red to blend with the brick. Comfortable wicker chairs graced both sides of the door, their cushions covered in bright flowered fabric that coordinated nicely with the rest of the furniture. Stacy, or more likely her mom, had redecorated since her last visit. All along the front were the rose bushes for which the *Castle*, actually named the *Blue Rose Bed & Breakfast*, was famous.

The wind picked up, blowing her hair across her face and sending a shiver down her spine. March in Boston was not yet time for roses. Though there was no snow on the ground, it still felt like winter. She hurried up the steps to get out of the wind just as the door opened.

"Megan!" Stacy's exuberant hug nearly knocked her over, which was hard to do given Megan stood six foot tall in her stocking feet. "Come in,come in!" She grabbed

Megan by the coat and practically dragged her into the house.

"My suitcase." Megan turned back but Stacy snagged it and rolled it inside, closing the door with a slam.

Stacy, only five foot two, with blonde hair and blue eyes, had always reminded Megan of Tinker Bell. Even more so now as she fluttered around. "I am so excited you're here."

"I can tell." Megan shrugged out of her coat and automatically turned to hang it on the coat rack to the left of the door.

"There's just so much going on," Stacy continued. "After a rather slow winter, the *Castle* is starting to fill up on weekends, and the summer months are practically all booked. But all that can wait. Come on back to the kitchen so we can talk while I make a few appetizers for happy hour."

Stacy turned and Megan followed, the Bed & Breakfast as familiar as her own home. A wide staircase ran along the right side of the hall up to the second then third floors. When they were little, Stacy's bedroom had been upstairs along with her parents', and her two brothers had shared the huge loft on the third floor. After everyone had grown and left, her parents had converted their home to a Bed & Breakfast, adding bathrooms and dividing the loft into two airy suites. When her parents retired and moved to Arizona, Stacy had used their room as another suite and had moved to the basement, which was just as roomy and well-appointed as the rest of the house.

Immediately to the left of the entryway was a small library with a desk and computer, complete with Wi-Fi connections. It allowed guests a little privacy and quiet. Next was a sitting room, open to the guests and housing a big screen TV and several sitting areas. Megan remembered the winter Stacy's parents had taken out the wall between that and the dining room, opening the space to accommodate more guests when needed.

Now they cut through the dining room and around the table, easily able to seat twenty. The table held a pretty arrangement of foliage, complementing the dark wood of the buffet and sideboard. Their childhood nickname of the *Castle* was totally appropriate given the size of the house itself, full of antique furniture and gilt trimmed pictures. The spacious gardens to the back, complete with gazebo, added to its appeal. And everything was spotless.

She followed Stacy through the half door into the kitchen. This was the one room of the house that had been completely modernized. State of the art appliances included a sub-zero refrigerator, six burner range and two ovens. Here, too, everything gleamed and the scent of rich coffee filled the air.

"How do you keep up with all this?" Megan asked.

"Sheesh, it's not like I do it," Stacy saucily replied as she reached above the counter and grabbed two coffee mugs. "You know how much I like housework." She handed Megan a cup and spoon then turned and grabbed a bottle of creamer from the fridge.

Megan laughed as she poured a goodly amount of creamer into her coffee and stirred. "If I remember right, your mom always made you keep your door closed, even if there wasn't any company. And she didn't even venture to the loft where Cal and Jeff slept."

Stacy's voice was muffled, head buried in the refrigerator. "I hate to say it, but we never changed. At least Cal and Jeff moved out after college." She pulled out a tray of cheese and salami, and another of pickles, tiny carrots and olives, setting them on the counter in front of Megan.

She automatically reached for a black olive, munching slowly, hoping having her mouth full would keep her from asking about Cal, Stacy's oldest brother and Megan's teenage crush.

Stacy dumped a tube of fancy crackers into a pottery bowl that was lined with a pretty embroidered napkin. "Help yourself." She shoved everything closer. "I know they don't feed you on airplanes anymore and," she paused, glancing at the clock, "what time did you leave California?"

Megan groaned. "Seven this morning. Even with the plane changes in Denver and Chicago, there wasn't enough time to grab anything." Stacking salami and cheese on a cracker, she munched happily as Stacy continued her preparations.

"You haven't started serving all meals, have you?" she asked.

Stacy shook her head. "Just breakfast, but not long ago I started having happy hour. Most of our guests come back from their meanderings around four or five to change before they go out for the evening. Well, at least in the summer that seems to be the pattern. Right now, the three registered couples told me they had late lunches while they were out sightseeing. So now, they're probably in for the night. They seem to enjoy having a little snack and a glass of wine."

She cocked her head to the side, and when Megan listened, she heard the television and a lot of yelling. Stacy smiled. "I dare say the ladies weren't as ready to return as the guys."

Megan sent her a questioning look.

Stacy sighed. "Honestly, Meggie. March Madness; college basketball?"

Megan shrugged.

"I can't believe you have lived this long, especially hanging around here with Cal and Jeff, and have no head for sports."

"I did watch the Super Bowl this year," Megan replied defensively.

"Only because you were on a date, as I recall from our texting." She raised a brow as only she could. "How is Brad, by the way?"

Megan snagged another piece of salami. "I wouldn't know. The Super Bowl marked not only the beginning and end of my foray into sports, but the end of our relationship, if you could even call it that." She had dated Brad for six months and finally asked herself *why?* She decided that was enough.

"And you never called?" Stacy grabbed two of the plates and swept around the counter. "Hold that thought, I'll be right back." Megan thought to help, so picked up the cracker bowl and followed Stacy into the dining room.

"Hi, everyone. This is my good friend, Megan." Stacy waved in her direction and Megan nodded in recognition of the 'hellos' from the couples sitting in the adjacent room. "Here's the wine. Please help yourself, but no throwing things at the TV. It's only a game."

"Only a game?" One of the guys echoed. "First time in years Iowa made it to the sweet sixteen."

"But you're from Chicago," Stacy replied.

"I know, but I thought about going to school in Iowa." He grinned as he stacked some of the snacks onto a plate and grabbed a napkin. A yell from his friends had him hurrying back to the TV.

"They're good for now. Come on," Stacy said as she went back into the kitchen, closing the top of the half door so they could talk in peace.

"You still like doing this, don't you?" Megan could tell her friend enjoyed her role as hostess, as she had when her folks first opened their home to strangers.

"I love it, but don't think you can change the subject so easily. What happened with Brad?"

Megan sipped her coffee before answering. "There was just no spark."

"But he was a doctor," Stacy exclaimed. "We were always going to marry doctors or lawyers, or international celebrities, remember?"

"Yes and here we are. You as the very congenial hostess of a very successful B&B, and me..." Her voice trailed off.

Her friend reached across the counter, her small hand covering Megan's. "What is it, Meggie? You said when you left Boston after college that you'd never come back. Yet here you are."

Megan scrunched up her face. Her parents had died when she was a teen. There had just been nothing here for her. But now, when push came to shove, the *Castle* was the only place she had to go.

"I quit my job," she said. "Or rather, my job quit me."

Stacy squeezed her hand, then spun around. "This calls for more than coffee." She grabbed a bottle from the cupboard and two shot glasses from another. Quickly she poured two shots, held one up and nodded to Megan to get the other.

Only Stacy, Megan thought, picking up the shot glass, tapping it against Stacy's and downing the clear liquid.

"God!" She gasped as liquid fire raced down her throat, hitting her near empty stomach with a splash. She nearly dropped the glass onto the counter.

"It gets better," Stacy said as she poured them each another shot. "Bottoms up." When Megan didn't immediately pick up her glass, Stacy added the inevitable, "Dare you."

She had no choice, and licked her lips after downing the shot, the peachy flavor lingering. When Stacy started to pour a third round, Megan put her hand over the glass. "No more; not until I get something more than crackers in my stomach. Besides, aren't you on duty?"

Stacy shrugged. "Not really. I serve an evening snack as a little plus, so it's not like they expect any special service. Actually we could go downstairs, but let me fix you some dinner first."

"No, you don't have to do that. Just no more shots." Megan turned the bottle around. "Cruzan peach rum?"

"Who's drinking that sissy stuff?" A deep voice came from the back porch just as the door opened. A tingle of awareness raced up Megan's spine. She didn't have to see his face to know it was Cal. A tall frame filled the doorway as he shrugged off his jacket.

His voice had always drawn her; deep and gravelly and totally seductive. She hadn't seen Stacy's brother since high school, and his gangly but athletic high school physique had certainly filled out in the years since. As her heart thudded erratically, she thought some things never changed. The crush she had all those years ago still morphed her back into a tongue-tied teenager.

"Well, well. If it isn't little Megan Sue, the fourth but unacknowledged Garrett kid. Hey, sis." He actually ruffled his sister's hair as he headed for the sink, his back now to Megan.

Which was just as well because she knew she was staring. Cal had been good looking in high school, but now he was devastatingly handsome. Completely opposite of Stacy's fair complexion and blonde features, Cal's hair was darkest brown, wavy and just to the shaggy side of too long. Broad shoulders tapered down to a trim waist. Tight jeans covered a butt that was…oh, so fine. The glimpse she had gotten of his face was all she had needed to fully recall his dark eyes, high cheek bones and strong chin, covered with dark stubble that was so sexy nowadays.

"Megan?" Stacy's voice broke through her reverie. Megan swallowed and forced her gaze from Cal's back. It was the one secret she had from Stacy, because how could she ever tell her best friend that she had the hots for her brother for the past fifteen years?

"What made you bring out the hard stuff, Stac?" Having dried his hands and tossed the towel aside, Cal turned around to lean against the counter, long legs crossed at the ankles and arms crossed over his chest. He was casually dressed in jeans and a button down shirt, and while his pose might appear just as relaxed, Megan knew he was always watchful.

"Megan quit her job," Stacy began, and Megan couldn't see correcting her.

With a *harrumph*, Cal reached over Stacy's head to the liquor cabinet and pulled down a different bottle. "Then you should be drinking this." He quickly poured shots, raised his in salute and downed it. Megan lifted hers to delicately sniff.

"No way." She set it back down. When Stacy shot her a questioning look, she added, "Do you remember the last time we drank tequila?"

11

Cal laughed when Stacy smacked him in the chest with her hand. "She just got here, Cal, don't be chasing her away so fast. Besides, what are you even doing here? Aren't you on duty?"

"It was quitting time so I just thought I'd stop by and see you." He gave her a grin that would stop the heartbeat of most women, but his sister was immune.

"In other words, you didn't bother going to the grocery store this week." She just shook her head and rummaged in the refrigerator, coming up with a package of pork chops. "I was planning on Jeff, but he at least called to say he had other plans, so there should be enough for your hollow leg." She began grabbing spices from the side cupboard and rubbing some into the meat. "But you have to start the grill and cook," she added.

Cal gave Megan a casual wink before stepping through the door onto the back deck. Megan wished it had been Jeff coming over. Although the brothers looked extremely alike, Jeff was just three years older than she, whereas Cal was five. Megan didn't know if it was the age difference or what, but Jeff had simply been her friend's older brother, whereas Cal had been her fantasy.

"Why did you have to tell him I quit my job?" Megan asked Stacy in a low voice.

"Well, you did, didn't you?"

"Not exactly." It wasn't something Megan wanted to get into at the moment.

For Stacy, the world was pretty much black and white. "Do you have a job?"

"No."

"Well there you go. Besides, you and Cal do the same thing so maybe he can find you a job in Boston." She dropped the wooden spoons she was using to toss a salad. "Would that not be absolutely fabulous; you back in Boston for good?"

Megan held up a hand to curb her enthusiasm. "If Cal is still a detective with BPD, we are so far from 'doing the same thing' as to be laughable."

"What do you do?" This from Cal as he came back inside.

Megan groaned. She simply did not want to have this conversation, with either of them actually.

"I'm an investigative reporter," she said.

Cal gave a bark of laughter. "You're right. Not even close." He grabbed the chops and was back outside before Megan had time to reply.

She would have liked to be offended, but she had said herself it wasn't the same. "Look, let's leave my history alone for the time being and you can tell me what's been going on here. How are your folks?"

"Dad seems to think his golf game is ready for the Senior Tour, and Mom is just Mom. They love Arizona and can't believe they waited so long before moving there." She paused before speculating, "I think Mom misses the people, though, and I wonder if she won't try and talk Dad into buying a house and opening a B&B there."

Megan laughed. "What about Jeff?" She and Stacy had shared newsy letters before phone texting came along, so she knew Jeff was still in the area.

"His tour business is going great guns," she said. The door slammed as Cal came back with the chops. The smell of grilled meat made Megan's stomach rumble.

"Yeah, but he'd better keep his nose clean this season. I'm tired of bailing him out of trouble." He put the plate of meat on the small table in the kitchen nook. "Soup's on."

Megan grabbed the water glasses Stacy had filled and slid onto one of the benches. Stacy followed with the salad and Cal sat across from them.

Cal dove into his dinner and neither Stacy nor he added to his comment. Considering Megan's own predicament, she wasn't going to pry. The rest of the meal was spent in casual conversation about the Inn's current guests and the lingering cold weather now that March was here.

As she removed the dinner plates, Stacy used her fresh apple pie to bribe Cal into fixing the leaky faucet, and Megan just laughed. Although he grumbled, which made

Megan laugh harder, he dragged in the tool box from the garage and had the drip fixed in no time. It was all part of the big brother act because she knew he would do anything for his baby sister.

After he left, she and Stacy cleaned up the kitchen, shut off the lights and went downstairs where the family living quarters were. Changing into pajamas and warm robes, they sat in the living room and talked well into the night.

"So you didn't quit, you got fired over a little story?" Stacy was outraged on Megan's behalf when she finally got the story out of her.

"It wasn't a little story, it was a major political upheaval. I had been working on it for weeks, but my boss said the evidence was sketchy and he wouldn't send it to the top floor editors to be approved for publishing. Then, within a week, the Mayor and other major government officials resigned, everything broke loose, and our newspaper didn't have the story. When the top editors jumped my boss, he blamed me, and they 'let me go'."

"Didn't you blow the whistle on your boss?"

Megan smiled. "I was trying to blow the whistle on the local government officials but there was no sense crying and pointing fingers inside the newspaper. My boss has been with the paper for too many years for them to listen to a relative newbie."

Stacy stood and stretched. "You can stay here for as long as you want, and we'll just find you something to write about in Boston. The west coast's loss is the east coast's gain."

Megan smiled at the reference. Many cities along the eastern seaboard considered themselves superior to the west coast. Perhaps it was their history.

Megan wasn't at all sure that investigative reporting was what she still wanted to do. Then again, crime scene investigation had been her career choice at one time and that hadn't worked out too well either. With a sigh, she hugged her friend good night and they both went their separate ways.

14

The guest room Stacy had shown Megan was large and the bed comfortable. White lacy curtains covered the safety windows that had been installed when the house had been updated. The patterned blue wallpaper was reminiscent of the past and complimented the antique chest of drawers and vanity. She crawled into bed, having no trouble falling to sleep. The old house creaked and groaned as everyone settled for the night, and if she dreamed at all, she didn't remember the next day.

Chapter 2

Thursday afternoon Cal stopped at the B&B to see his sister. At least that was his story even though he knew Stacy was gone.

He was having trouble admitting to himself that seeing Megan again had floored him. She had been cute in high school, but since he was five years older, their paths hadn't crossed except at home and he certainly hadn't dated her. Once he went away to college, he hadn't come home much. And once she left for college, she hadn't come back at all.

Somewhere in the past fifteen years, she had grown into a beautiful woman. Where once her long legs had made her awkward, they now perfectly complimented her curvy hips and well-endowed chest. Her hair curled around her face with highlights that looked like liquid gold and her eyes still glittered with mischief.

And believe me, she and Stacy had created havoc in his and Jeff's lives growing up. Megan's parents had lived close enough that they all went to the same school, but since John and Rebecca Anderson had both been archeologists, they were frequently gone on excavations and Megan would stay with Stacy. When her parents had been killed in a cave-in in Argentina, Megan had come to live with the Garrett family full time. Thus his acknowledgement of her as the fourth Garrett sibling.

No way did he think of her as a sister now. His body had come to full wakefulness when he had seen her and it had been extremely hard to act nonchalant during dinner. He had never experienced such an instant attraction before and his fact-focused, detective brain wanted him to dissect and theorize. He stayed away for two weeks trying to forget her, but she had even managed to invade his dreams. All because of a single dinner and a little chitchat.

Now, he opened the porch door and stomped his boots on the throw rug, wondering if he was crazy to even think what he was thinking about his sister's BFF.

"Anyone here?" he called as he stepped through the doorway into the kitchen.

"Oh." Megan spun around from the center island, hands flattened over her chest and eyes wide. "You scared the sh...you scared me. How did you get in here?"

Cal dangled his keys.

"You have a key?" Her voice shook and he wondered why she was so nervous.

"Well, yeah. I used to live here, you know. Besides, I'm a cop. I'd have little trouble getting in without a key." He grinned at her and her shoulders finally relaxed.

"Where's Stac?" He reached around her and grabbed a chunk of cheese from the tray she was preparing. The faint scent of her perfume tickled his senses, reminding him of warm summer days when the roses were in full bloom.

His chest brushed her arm and he heard her suck in a breath. He turned his head slightly and gazed into eyes the color of emeralds, pupils dilated, and it was like drowning in a dark, sensual sea. *Geez, blooming roses and sensual seas; what was he thinking?*

Plundering those dark seas with her, that's what he was thinking.

Cal mentally shook himself. Megan wasn't the type you picked up at a bar and casually took home to bed. He wasn't sure how he knew that, but his instincts had him taking a step back at the same time she did.

"It's Thursday and Stacy said it was date night, though she was going to cancel because I was here, but I told her to go." Megan was rambling and Cal smiled. Maybe she was nervous because she felt their attraction, too.

"Who's she dating?"

Megan came away from the refrigerator with a tray of veggies, her lips pinched in silence.

"You don't know?" he asked. "She didn't tell you?"

17

More like the Megan he knew from the past, she snorted. "Like I would tell you."

Using her hip, she bumped open the half door and disappeared with the food, only to return a few minutes later. "You're the cop," she threw his words back at him, "you figure it out."

She didn't give him time for a comeback as she took the other plates of food into the dining room. He felt her purposely avoiding him as she scooted around the far side of the island to grab the bottles of wine that were open and breathing.

When she once again returned, he lightly grabbed her arm when she started to sail by. "Are you done?"

She opened her mouth, then slowly shut it again. She glanced at the sink, the stove, anywhere but at him.

"Ok, so I know who she's dating. I was just razing you, wondering if the girls' secret society was still in force." He dropped his hand. "Well, since she's not here, there won't be a home cooked meal, so grab your coat. I'll take you out."

"I can get my own dinner," she replied.

"Yeah, but since you got fired from your job, I'll treat you tonight."

Her mouth dropped open and she started to shake her head in denial.

"Stacy told me." He wiggled his brows. "She tells me everything."

* * *

She tells me everything. Cal's words echoed in Megan's head as he drove around the Boston Common and headed toward Chinatown. It was definitely a good thing she had never said anything to Stacy about her crush on Cal, or how she had felt when he showed up that first night. Unlike the benign feelings Brad had evoked, when she had seen Cal, sexual awareness had literally slammed into her, stealing her breath and her thought processes, just like now.

18

She fidgeted with her purse strap then made herself still her hands. She was thirty years old, for Pete's sake. There was no reason to be nervous. After all, it was only Cal. That didn't help a bit, especially with the chemistry between them. *She* felt it, anyway, but something in his gaze and his husky tone when he spoke told her the feeling wasn't one-sided.

She glanced his way, his gaze concentrating on the road ahead. Early evening in Boston wasn't a time when you wanted to be driving, unless you had been born and raised there. Or unless you were a cop, she amended, grabbing the handle above the door as Cal swerved around a car and did a quick right onto a side street.

"Where's the light and siren?" she quipped.

He flashed a grin. "They don't always let me play with the toys." He expertly slid the big F-150 into a parking spot right next to the South Street Diner, a favorite hangout for locals and tourists alike. When she got out and met him at the curb he held out his hand. "Got any change?"

She shook her head in disbelief. "You offer me dinner because you think I'm broke, but I have to pay parking?" She dug out her coin purse and shook the contents into her palm.

"Guys don't carry little coin purses." He plucked some quarters and inserted them into the meter.

"I know guys who do."

He snorted. "Yeah, in California. I'll bet you know guys who wore heels and dresses, too." He took her elbow and led her into the diner.

"That is such a…an East coast thing to say."

He took her coat and hung it on a peg beside their booth, then slid in across from her. "Hey, Boston has a long history of macho fighting men who weren't afraid to speak up."

Megan shook her head. "We are not going to rehash two hundred years of history over dinner. You know how I feel about that."

He just grinned. "There's always the chance of converting you, Tory."

19

Megan didn't answer as the waitress appeared at their table. She ordered a soda and Cal got coffee.

"I just don't understand how anyone can grow up in Boston and have no interest in, or sense of history," Cal continued as if she hadn't said anything.

He was right, of course. She *knew* Boston's history as it had been hammered into her since childhood. She just didn't have any real interest in the distant past. She knew that was particularly ironic since her father had taught archeology at Boston College. He had always told her that things from the past would always affect the present, and therefore it was important to not only preserve, but study.

Upon moving in with the Garrett family fifteen years ago, she had found that she did appreciate antique furnishings and their history, just as long as she had hot running water and electricity.

"Are you turning into Jeff?" She asked. Jeff was Cal and Stacy's middle brother, and had an avid interest in Boston history. So much so that he had started his own tour company here.

Cal grinned. "No, but it's my home and therefore I take an interest."

When the waitress appeared to take their order, she flirted openly with Cal, who appeared to return her interest. Megan could feel her eyes narrow, even though she had no claim to him.

"Gosh, this place brings back memories," she interrupted to say, crossing her legs under the table and *accidently* kicking Cal. "Sorry." She smiled when his gaze came back to her, but it was enough of an interruption for the waitress to leave.

The South Street Diner was originally built in 1947 to serve local factory workers. Over the years, it had become a local landmark as an after-hours destination for residents and visitors. There were only half a dozen booths, their glittering blue vinyl bench seats matching the bar stools along the counter.

The neighborhood around the Diner had evolved from shoe and hand bag producing factories to an artist community and student Mecca. Though listed as a "must see' for tourists, it was still a favorite of long time Bostonians.

Cal gave her a wicked grin. "My memories include rescuing you and Stacy one late night when you told the folks you were going to a movie and came down here instead."

Megan huffed. "It's not like you never said you were going one place and really went elsewhere."

"I'm a guy," he replied.

"Well, that explains it," she said, hoping the sarcasm would be clear in her tone.

His eyes narrowed. "You two were fourteen and trying to attract boys, then got scared when some college apes hit on you."

Megan recalled the incident all too clearly, but tried to rationalize. "That was half a lifetime ago, speaking of history."

Their food arrived and Megan bit into her juicy cheeseburger. "Oh my God, this tastes so good."

"Stacy hasn't been feeding you?"

Megan shrugged. "I'm not so much into organic and healthy. I love red meat, fried food and dessert."

"My kind of gal," Cal quipped, his gaze locking with hers.

* * *

The days seemed to fly by and stand still at the same time. Contradictory for sure, but that was how Megan felt. She spent her days online job hunting and even had an interview with one of the smaller papers in town, but they hadn't gotten back to her. She had written a few general pieces on contract with the *Boston Globe*, but the pay wasn't much. She wanted to look for an apartment, but didn't want to dip into her savings. Stacy kept telling her she didn't need to go house hunting. Megan loved her friend dearly, but really felt she needed her own space.

In the meantime, she helped Stacy with breakfast and the evening happy hour. Sometimes, she did laundry when her friend was out shopping for the next round of guests and at the moment was elbow deep in dish water, finishing the last of the wine glasses that didn't go in the dishwasher.

"Jeff's right behind me," Stacy said now as she came in the back door. "I hope you're decent."

"I hope she's not." Jeff's laughter preceded his appearance as he balanced two grocery bags and elbowed the back door shut. He quickly set the bags on the counter and grabbed Megan in a bear hug, lifting her completely off the ground and giving her a sloppy kiss on the cheek.

"God, you look fantastic!" He clutched her hands and held them out to the sides before dropping one and twirling her around in a circle.

Megan laughed. She felt just as close to Jeff as she did to Stacy, although for different reasons. Whereas she and Stacy had shared clothes, secrets about boys and makeup, Jeff had helped her pass Algebra and had explained why high school boys acted so dumb most of the time. Of course, he never included himself in that description.

"How are you, Jeff?" she finally managed. "You look good." Jeff wore his hair long, pulled back at the nape, and he had the classic Garrett male looks – dark and lethally handsome.

"Great; better than great now that I've seen you. I have the perfect job for you."

Megan shot Stacy a look and her friend had the decency to blush.

"Well, he asked what you were doing."

All through dinner, Jeff regaled her with stories of his tours. He did the scenic Boston Common, Public Garden and state house tour. He also narrated the walk along the Freedom Trail that included Paul Revere's house, the Old North Church and Copp's Hill Burial Ground. Megan laughed at some of the absurd questions tourists would ask.

"I need something new and different," Jeff continued. "I've been doing some research on our house and old

McCluer, the guy who built it back in the eighteenth century."

"Really? Did you find anything new?" There had always been stories about the original owners of the house. When they were kids, Jeff and Cal had thought they were related to the McCluers therefore had to have privateers on the Garrett family tree.

"The history and owners of the house can be traced with public records, so not much is new there. But I found an old tome at the historical society and there seems to be some discrepancies as to what happened after the daughter of the manor disappeared."

"Remember how we always thought we saw Laurie's ghost after the boys told us that story?" Stacy asked. "We'd scream and they'd come running."

Megan vividly remembered the ghostly form floating down the stairs or lingering at dusk by the gazebo. She also recalled how many time she had dreamed about her, and how the ghostly presence had appeared pleading, asking Megan for something she didn't understand. Thankfully, those dreams had ceased when she left for college.

Jeff's voice cut into her musing. "Anyway, that's the story we're going to portray with our new tour, *To the River's Edge*."

"It'll be great advertising for the B&B, too," Stacy chimed in. "Jeff's people will meet here for the start of the tour and we'll serve tea in the sitting room, or porch, depending on the weather."

Megan nodded, but then questioned, "How are you going to make it interesting enough just telling a story?"

"It's a walking tour, so we start the story here, talk as we weave around a few of the back streets to the river, where re-enactors will tell the tale as a play. Then we end down at O'Brien's Pub. By incorporating our B&B and O'Brien's, not only do I make money, but so do Stacy and Patrick O'Brien."

"Well, I wish you luck," Megan said as she stood to clear the dinner dishes.

"You were great in theater," Jeff needled. "You would make a great Laurie Elizabeth Victoria McCluer."

"That's a mouthful," she laughed then shook her head. "I don't really remember the story, and you know how I feel about all the historical gibberish that goes on during tourist season."

Jeff raised a brow. "Are you saying—?"

"Not you," Megan immediately backpedaled. "I know the history you tell is authentic, but some guides trying to make a buck tell a crock of you know what; things that never really happened. And what about those who dress up as historical figures then charge people to have their picture taken with them? Many people are more interested in making money than telling Boston's history as it really happened."

"Exactly. That's why this new tour will be so exciting. You have to be part of it," Jeff cajoled. "At least think about it."

Although she really didn't see herself in a long dress and Haymaker Bonnet, carrying a candle lantern around in the dark, she dreamed about it that night. It was the vivid type of dream where she really thought she was awake. Laurie McCluer was walking along the river, beckoning her. When she approached, the young woman held out her hands in supplication, but didn't speak, although her eyes beseeched her. Then she simply disappeared.

* * *

Since Friday was a day many people arrived at the B&B for the weekend, Stacy would often take Thursday night off. She and her current fling, Matthew, would go out because as Stacy said, if they stayed in, she invariably worked. But within minutes after they left, like clockwork, Cal showed up at the back door. Megan sometimes wondered if he didn't sit in his truck around the corner, waiting for Matt's car to go by. Except for that first time, he didn't use Stacy as an excuse, so Megan knew he was actually there to see her.

They had fallen into an easy comradery, sometimes going out to eat and sometimes Cal would bring steaks to cook on the grill, explaining that it was a 'guy thing' when she would tell him they could cook something inside.

She certainly couldn't complain that he was all male, and every time she saw him the tingles would start from her toes up and her heart would beat just a little faster. Though their banter was easy and she felt comfortable with him, there was still something simmering, hot and volatile, just below the surface. She sometimes questioned holding herself in check, but was old fashioned enough to want the man to make the first move.

But he hadn't put a move on her and she wondered if it was because she was Stacy's friend and he still thought of her as fourteen. More often than not, after Cal left, she would go to bed achy and dreaming of what it would be like to make love to him. Or at least have him kiss her so she would know whether her feelings were one sided.

Tonight seemed like every other Thursday. After dinner they remained at the table, Cal nursing a beer. She fiddled with her glass of wine.

"What is it?" He asked, his brows coming together and his tone making her remember he was a detective and would find out what he wanted to know whether she told him or not. And she certainly wasn't going to tell him her current thoughts.

Instead, she broached another topic on her mind. "When you were living at home, did you ever hear of anything…peculiar?"

He actually snorted. "You mean like ghosts in the attic? Perhaps Laurie McCluer roaming around looking for her beloved?"

Her look must have made him rethink his sarcasm. "This house has been around for over two hundred years. We thought it was great when we moved in, and Jeff and I scoured every inch from basement to attic for anything that might confirm the legend associated with it. But we felt nothing; heard nothing; stumbled across nothing." He shrugged. "It's just a house."

25

Megan thought otherwise, but if she was the only one having dreams… "What about Stacy?"

"Ha. You and Stac always thought a prince would come riding up and carry you off. There's your fantasy."

She scowled. Apparently her friend really did tell her brother everything. Deciding to deflect the conversation from herself, she said, "You never have said much about what you do, although I know you're a cop."

"Detective," he corrected, then shrugged. "Believe it or not, Boston is a relatively quiet town, and at the moment I have no open cases. Knock on wood. But now that the Sox season has started, things tend to get rowdy for the beat patrol."

"Any undercover work?"

He grinned. "Trying to find a story? Whatever happened to the crime scene career?"

Megan pulled a face. "When I studied criminology, there were so many subfields to choose from, but that one had too much gore. I did enjoy the research and trying to figure out the secrets, so I turned to investigative reporting, mostly in technology fields."

"That sounds totally boring."

She laughed. "Not when you start looking at the latest technology companies, the subterfuge of buying and selling new innovative software, and cybercrime."

"Geek stuff."

Megan got up to retrieve the bottle of wine, and when she turned back around, Cal had moved right behind her. He casually circled her waist with his big hands. She was almost as tall as his six foot two, and fit very nicely in his arms.

"I prefer the hands on approach." When she just stood there and didn't say anything, Cal figured she didn't mind his advance. He had watched her lips as she ate, and every bite she took had caused his groin to tighten. He could no longer deny that he was attracted to her, not that he ever had. He just hadn't made a move because, well, she was Stacy's best friend.

"Put down the bottle, Megan," he whispered as his lips brushed her forehead. She was clutching it against her chest and it was severely tampering his attempts at getting closer.

She turned slightly and set the bottle on the counter, still not talking. But her eyes spoke volumes. The color had darkened and she gazed at him with curiosity. He decided to satisfy both of them. He took her lips gently at first, but at her response, he quickly deepened the kiss. She was sweet and hot, and although he knew she couldn't be innocent, she still kissed with the exuberance of youth.

Cal wasn't innocent, not at all. He'd had his fair share of affairs in his lifetime, but everything about Megan made him feel like he was eighteen again. Her lighthearted laugh, her sense of humor, even the fact that she could almost out eat him had him craving more than a kiss.

She pushed slightly against him, making him come up for air. Was she pushing him away? He had thought the vibes between them meant she wanted the same thing he did.

"No?" He tilted his head to the side, but didn't release her.

She bit her bottom lip and it drove him crazy, but he still didn't advance. It was up to her.

When a slow smile curved her lips and her eyes twinkled, he started breathing again.

"Yes," she whispered, stepping closer so her breasts brushed his chest as her lips took his with even more heat.

Kissing Cal was everything she had always fantasized it would be; probably more. His arms were tight bands around her, his mouth hot and hard against her yielding lips. Just when her legs threatened to buckle, he spun her around and pushed her up against the wall, never loosening his lips from hers.

She curled her arms around his shoulders, hanging on tight as he grabbed her butt, hiking her up and nestling his hips tight against the juncture of her thighs. Her legs automatically wrapped around his waist.

She gasped for breath when he finally released her lips, but her reprieve was short-lived as he began a foray down

27

her neck to the open vee of her shirt. His tongue licked along the lace of her bra, making her shiver, which caused her hips to push against his.

He groaned, hips gyrating.

"No," she whispered, and when he didn't stop, she placed both hands to the sides of his face and gently lifted his head until their eyes met. His held a question and Megan wasn't sure how to answer it.

She liked Cal, liked him a lot. There had been a connection between them from the first and his kisses drove her through the roof. He had a high sense of humor and more than that, he was a very caring person. One had to be, if one was a cop.

And therein lay the problem. He would take care of her if she allowed it, but she had been independent since high school and it was beginning to grate on her that she didn't have a job or her own place. For now, her one time fantasy would have to remain that unless she could come to him on more equal terms. Unwrapping her legs from around his hips, she slid to a stand.

"Too soon," she whispered as he released her.

"We're not done," he replied as he gave her one last, lingering kiss then turned to leave. As she closed the door behind him, she sighed. If she wanted more kisses, even if she couldn't live on kisses alone, there was only one answer. She had to get a job.

Chapter 3

"Augh…h…h…h!"

The scream pierced the quiet, causing Megan to jump as a shiver streaked down her spine. Glancing quickly to the right then left, she saw nothing out of the ordinary in the bright afternoon sunlight.

"Seriously, Jeff?" She turned to her companion, who was doubled over with laughter.

"It made you jump," he snickered.

She smacked his arm with her fist.

Rubbing his bicep, he took a step back. "Actually, it's pretty effective at night, especially when there's no moon."

Megan glanced back to the river, where the blue water glistened with barely a ripple, though she knew a swift current flowed just beneath the surface. Her gaze caught the movement of a scull midstream, cutting swiftly through the water, the eight men rowing in perfect sync. It didn't seem like the backdrop for some murderous happenstance.

Just as she turned back, a young girl peeked out from behind the giant oak tree that stood at the edge of the bank. She waved, and when Jeff beckoned, she trotted over to where they stood.

"How was that?"

"Sounded great, Toni," Jeff told her. "Just make sure you keep it loud and draw it out as long as you can." He turned back to Megan. "This is Toni Lang. Toni, meet Megan Anderson, our newest recruit."

"Great to have you on board." Toni grabbed Megan's hand with both of hers and shook it vigorously.

"I didn't say I would do it," Megan said defensively, trying to extract her hand from Toni's.

"Oh, you have to. It's going to be ever so much fun." The girl, who looked about fourteen, practically bounced in a circle.

"I thought you did authentic tours." Megan narrowed her gaze at Jeff, who was still smiling after making her jump in reaction to the scream. "This is sensationalism."

"Do you remember the story?" he retorted.

She shrugged. She wasn't about to tell him that talking about the legend and being back in the house had caused her dreams to begin again. When she had first moved in with the Garrett family, the boys had told her and Stacy the story, sitting in the gazebo while rain pounded the roof and lightning cut through the night. Now she was again dreaming about being dragged into the river by the British, and often thought she heard voices in the hallways of the huge house. Some days she felt she hadn't slept at all, but had spent the night trying to decipher what Laurie wanted from her.

She tried to focus on what Jeff was saying.

"From all my research in the historical archives," he continued, "McCluer's daughter disappeared one night right about here, and then strange things started happening all along the Charles River and the port."

"Like?"

"Like a cache of British coins and a crate of Ferguson Breech-Loader rifles disappeared…bodies."

Megan had heard about those Boston treasures that had yet to be found. "You mean the story is true?"

"Well, I can't authenticate if bodies actually washed ashore," Jeff said with a shrug.

"So it is a ghost story?"

Instead of answering her, Jeff said, "Did you know this all used to be McCluer's land, from the house clear down to the river. They had a wharf and a warehouse there," he pointed, "and a dirt road ran from here to the Commons where McCluer had additional warehouses and his offices."

"Since that is all well and good, but rather boring for tourists, you're going to play on the idea of a ghost, aren't you?" Megan came right back to where they started.

"Boston's history is full of legends and ghosts. Who's to say there can't be one more?"

A shiver ran down Megan's back. She wasn't sure she wanted to immerse herself in history, especially something so close to home, yet she needed a job.

She sighed, knowing she was caving. "Give me the story."

Jeff grinned, handing over a dog eared stack of papers held together with a large red crab binder clip embossed with the words, 'Don't be crabby in Boston.'

* * *

It happened a very long time ago, when the mist still curled up the bank of the river and the silence echoed against the shore. Few houses had yet been built along the gentle curve of the water, for people appeared to like the safety offered by the closeness of town. There, houses were stacked tightly together, along streets almost too narrow to allow carriages to pass one another.

Laurie Elizabeth Victoria McCluer, however, lived high on a hill overlooking that magnificent Charles River. Her father was a wealthy tea merchant and without being pretentious, still liked to let his friends and acquaintances know that he had made a name for himself in the town of Boston. Their home was large and spacious, with a wide stairway, mahogany banister and a crystal chandelier that her father had imported from England.

Captain McCluer and his dear wife, Victoria, after whom Laurie was partially named, enjoyed entertaining, and visiting dignitaries could often be found gracing the flower gardens on the estate, or waltzing in the ballroom which covered the entire second floor of the house. Even when tensions arose and tempers grew short between residents of the colony of Boston and the soldiers sent from England to keep the peace, the McCluer family paid no heed.

Mrs. McCluer continued to entertain the wives of local merchants, as well as the few wives of British soldiers who had traveled with their husbands. Together, they would have tea among her roses, or settle into spacious chairs in the front parlor for an afternoon soiree. Oftentimes, Mrs. McCluer would request Laurie Elizabeth's presence, for she had a pure voice when raised in song, and of course, was Mrs. McCluer's pride and joy. Laurie did not mind entertaining her mother's friends, but she sincerely wished the British soldiers' wives were not in attendance. They tended to look down their noses, as though better than the McCluers, and Laurie had heard them whisper about the 'ignorant colonials'. Yet they were willing to accept the hospitality of her parent's home.

Laurie was all of eighteen years old, and considered herself a woman, even if her parents did not. She also had very definite ideas of what should be happening in Boston and the other colonies, and wasn't afraid to express herself. Of course, because of her gender, she had no voice in the politics of the day, so her opinions could only be spoken quietly in her father's study when they discussed the dissension. Even more secretly, her friends would gather down on the embankment where only the river overheard their feverishly whispered arguments for independence and their impassioned speeches of what they would do if they were in charge of the Commonwealth.

More and more Bostonians began to resent the presence of the British. Secrecy abounded, and oftentimes Laurie suspected that even the servants were divided between their loyalties, although her father paid them well enough to keep their silence. Her father made a very good living importing tea, along with other English items to the colonies, but he was in reality a colonist first, and his heart belonged to the Americas. In order to keep informed about the British troop movements and to provide protection for the activities of the Sons of Liberty, he kept up the pretense of being a Tory and stayed on good terms with Governor Hutchinson.

Laurie sincerely believed that her mother was the only member of the McCluer household who did not know where her husband's loyalties lie. This was no fault of her *mother's, for she loved her husband fiercely. She just did not have a head for politics, and simply enjoyed people, regardless of nationality, religion, or family origins.*

Now, you have the background, except for one missing character in the person of Laurie Elizabeth's betrothed. Mr. Logan Mallory, a most handsome young man who attended Harvard University, came from a very well-known and respected family in Charleston, South Carolina. Laurie had first met Logan when he began assisting her father at the docks and in the investment house where he conducted his business. She fell quickly in love, as he did with her, and they were promised to be married in the spring.

Much has been written about this time of our nation's history, and Boston was right in the thick of the conflict. While the general history is well known, rumors still fly and housemaids whisper behind their hands if you dare to mention Laurie Elizabeth and her betrothed -- handsome, Mr. Mallory. Their story is one of unrequited love, mystery and intrigue, where only the river really knows what became of them, and it silently glides past their point of parting without disclosing its secrets.

It was not a night like any other, for the summer rains had caused the river to swell against its banks and course wildly towards the Bay. Sailors were cautioned not to try to traverse her currents by small skiff, and any man foolhardy enough to think he could swim her width on a night such as this would only be asking to meet his Maker. Or the devil, as the case may be.

The small group who sat quietly beneath the huge oak by the bank felt relatively safe. Thinking no British ship or soldiers would venture this far, they could contemplate their next escapade. They were not the Sons of Liberty. Being of younger years, and some of them female, they did not quite understand their place as the hands of destiny tugged their hearts and minds in different directions. It is said of this night, though, that their arguments for forcing the British soldiers to leave their beloved Boston were quite adamant, and that Logan Mallory's voice rose loud and clear above the rest.

"We must not allow them to tell us how to live our lives!" It is reported he proclaimed, a clinched fist against his heart. "I, for one, am most willing to give my life for the freedoms we have." And all among him cheered his courage and admired his spirit, raising their hands to his in a show of unity.

Laurie's eyes must have also glowed with a rebellious spirit as she gazed adoringly at her betrothed. She not only loved him for his bearing and his family name -- and because he was the most handsome young man in the colony -- but she admired him greatly for his nobility in the face of such grave danger. But, perhaps because of her gender, and her loving but protective father, she naively thought she would love Logan forever and that they would live happily ever after. Surely no harm would come to them, and most certainly the British would leave soon enough, allowing the people of Boston to resume their quiet lives.

As their friends departed, leaving the young couple alone in the night by the wide, churning waters, Laurie could not have known the danger that lurked just around the bend in the river. For as secretive as they thought their meetings were, someone had betrayed them.

Her friends later spoke sorrowfully of hearing Laurie scream, her frightened voice echoing eerily against the fog floating on the water. Several of them raced back to the oak tree only to find young Logan knocked unconscious to the ground and Laurie nowhere in sight. As silently as it had come, the fog disappeared and the moon shone across the water. Yet nowhere in the moonlight could they see a body or a boat, or any semblance of conveyance which could have come and robbed them of one of their own.

Logan was beside himself, and raced along the bank yelling for his beloved Laurie. If not for friends restraining him, he might very well have flung himself into the raging waters in search of her. Surely his heart sank to the bottom of that muddy current, and his tears mixed with the misty spray. Inconsolable, he refused to come away from the slippery banks, and his friends stood vigil through the long, dark night as he continued to curse the river for taking her, yelling and sobbing her name in supplication. Finally, he drew into himself for failing to protect her from harm.

The cold, gray dawn crept up the river -- no sun shone this day, no white clouds reflected against the usual blue of the water. A silent rain, seeping its cold, wet fingers through their clothes, wrapped their hearts in sorrow. His friends could do no more, and one by one said their farewells to Logan who stood still as death by the spot where his Laurie had been taken. He could not acknowledge their solace, nor could he overcome the anger that had steadily overtaken his heart and mind. It soaked into his body as the rain had, shutting down his senses until that was all there was.

There was much speculation as to why Laurie was taken, and by whom, and it is unfortunate that no one had the courage to investigate until the mystery was solved. Both the Bostonians and the British blamed the other, for the colonists would never admit that they had not been able to protect the river and one of their own. The British, still being outnumbered at this time, did not want to start a conflict they had no hope of winning. Whispered accounts, however accurate, blamed the British, stating kidnapping as a ploy to make Mr. McCluer comply with the specifications of the British government on his tea business. Others -- Tories, it is said -- say Laurie was taken by colonists who were angered because McCluer did business with the British, but those closest to the family knew this to be the most vile of rumors.

Of poor Logan Mallory, even less is known. He disappeared that morning, never to be heard of by the people of Boston again. But very strangely, mishaps occurred to any British officer, ship, dingy, or sailor who dared to pass near the bend in the River where his beloved Laurie had disappeared. Drownings happened with frightening regularity and many a body washed ashore with a bullet hole in the chest.

Romantic young girls nearly swooned thinking that perhaps handsome Logan Mallory was avenging his lover's death. Idealistic young rebels toasted his daring in the taverns, and bravely boasted their courage as being as great as his.

Of course, you must realize that this is all hearsay, for none now were alive on that fateful day, and the story has been handed down by trusted household servant, parlor maid, or stable boy. But all agree Laurie Elizabeth Victoria McCluer's death, and Mr. Logan Mallory's disappearance are tragedies of the highest degree, and hearts weep for a love that could never be.

For those who believe, however, it is said that on some nights, when the moon is full and a low mist rolls in from the Bay, you can hear their voices down by the river, their laughter rising above the gentle flow of the current and the soft lapping of waves against the shore. And if you know where to find the old oak tree, you may even catch a glimpse of the two of them, hands raised in unison, voices echoing the cry for liberty.

* * *

The group sat around the table, each with a printed script as Jeff reviewed the parts to be played. Megan had read the story and wondered if it was Jeff's own work. In addition to his love of history, he had always had a flair for the dramatic, whether it was theatre or writing. He had taken a simple legend and woven factual history throughout to make an intriguing story.

That story, now in script form, had the narrator's part and the parts where the re-enactors would be speaking. Even if the audience didn't know Boston's history, the story would give them a factual view of the times with just enough drama and mystery to make it interesting. Besides, ending a tour at a pub was always the key to success.

Since the tour started at the B&B, as the story started at the McCluer's house, Stacy volunteered to portray Mrs. McCluer.

"I'll be serving drinks as the tour people arrive anyway," she said, "so I might as well continue 'acting' when the narrator starts."

Jeff said, "I'll be narrating the story until we all get a feel for the parts, but Megan will also be dressed for the time period and will help me out."

There were about a dozen other young people there who Megan hadn't officially met yet. Only Toni, who would be portraying Laurie, because according to Jeff, she could scream the loudest and longest.

"Dress rehearsal tomorrow," Jeff said. "We'll meet here half an hour before sunset. I want to do it just as it'll be done for real, and that means in the dark."

Megan shivered, glad that she wasn't doing the tour alone.

* * *

Cal arrived to find Megan walking around the sitting room in a long skirt and petticoats. The waist was pinched in over a flared skirt that reached the floor and puffed sleeves offset her creamy shoulders. The outfit somehow made her more feminine than had she been in leggings and a loose sweater hanging off her shoulders.

His wolf whistle had Megan spinning around, skirt swirling. She instantly responded to his grin, dipping into a curtsy that gave him a tantalizing view of breasts surrounded by lace.

He doffed an imaginary hat, bowed and was just about to sweep her into his arms for a kiss when he saw his sister.

"So, Jeff's roped you into his act as well," he said instead. "I like the dust mop." He tapped the gathered lace cap she wore as he turned to go back the way he had come, to the kitchen and fridge where he hoped to find a beer. As expected, the girls followed.

"The whole thing starts here at the McCluer residence," Stacy told him as she fluffed out her skirt. "Do you think I need more petticoats?" she asked.

Cal ignored her question. He had found over the years that any question a woman asked regarding fashion was the same as asking 'does this make my hips look fat.' A guy couldn't win.

"Thought you had a date with what's-his-name."

Stacy glared and Megan pinched her lips together to keep from laughing.

"As a matter of fact, *Matt* will be here any minute. He's agreed to critique the tour."

Cal frowned. "You're doing it tonight?" *Damn.* He had barely made it through the week, constantly thinking about the way Megan had kissed him. His schedule was never nine to five and he worked more nights than days, so Thursday was about the only night he managed to see her, mainly because it was Stacy's night away from the house. Usually, but it appeared that tonight would not be the night for him.

"Well, are you cooking dinner?"

"Calvin Michael Garrett! I am not your mother."

Cal loved to antagonize his sister as she was so easy to bait. He couldn't resist one more jab. "I know you're not. She did my laundry, too."

It was a good thing she only had a hot pad in her hand because it went sailing past his left ear.

"Good grief, you two. Some things haven't changed in all these years." Megan just shook her head at their antics.

But when Cal looked her way, he felt electricity shoot through him as her eyes twinkled. *Oh hell yeah,* things had definitely changed. Only his ringing phone brought him back to reality. Other than Stacy, who stood in front of him, and Jeff, who had just walked in the back door, his phone rarely rang except for work.

"Gotta go," he said, turning toward the door, his back to his siblings. Catching Megan's eye, he gave an almost imperceptible tilt of his head toward the door as he answered his phone with a curt, "Garrett."

The door slammed behind him and his boots crunched on the gravel as he walked towards his truck, but his senses picked up the soft sound of much lighter steps and he turned as he shut off and pocketed the phone.

An old fashioned shawl covered her shoulders and she held her dress up slightly so that he saw she wore sneakers. She looked so damned cute that when she stepped closer, a question in her gaze, he didn't hesitate.

Knowing he had only a moment, he reached out and pulled her close, his mouth slanting across hers to capture any protest she might have made. He needn't have worried as she immediately responded to his kiss.

"Thursday is supposed to be our night," he whispered roughly against her brow, then kissed a path back to the corner of her mouth.

"I know, but I needed a job," she replied before she turned her head slightly and sealed his lips with hers.

Cal groaned.

She finally pushed him away, her hands lingering on his chest. "I thought you had to work?"

Cal dropped his hands. "Shit." She could make him forget even his work, and as always the Captain had wanted him in the office half an hour ago.

Chapter 4

Megan's feet pounded the asphalt of the running lane as it curved along the outer edge of the Charles Esplanade. Ear buds in and IPod cranked up, she was oblivious to other joggers, walkers and babies pushed in strollers. She kept her eyes straight ahead and tried not to think, especially about last night and Jeff's first practice tour of *To the River's Edge*. But she couldn't entirely block her thoughts.

She hadn't slept a wink after it was over, which was why she was up at dawn running as though all the ghosts of hell were on her heels. She squinted as the sun made its appearance on the horizon. She hadn't remembered her sunglasses as it was dark when she left the house. Now, she thought about turning around so the sun was at her back, but she'd only done a quarter of her workout and wanted to get her full miles in. Plus running was supposed to keep her from thinking.

That wasn't working this morning, unfortunately, and her mind drifted back over last night. No one else had commented on the weird green haze along the river, or about the eerie keening sound long after Toni's effective scream had faded and the re-enactors had headed for the pub. She had tried subtly to inquire about the haze and sound effects, but Jeff said there had been nothing other than a faulty candle lantern. No one said anything about what she was sure *she* had seen. Cal had told her there were no ghosts and she hadn't mentioned her dream or last night's weirdness to Stacy because she didn't want to worry her friend. Still--

Whoop, whoop! The sharp, loud bleep of a siren directly behind her caused her to lose her footing and stumble, quickly grabbing a park bench. Before she could catch her balance, she was grabbed from behind and held tightly against a very hard chest.

"Christ, I'm sorry! I didn't think …"

The arms loosened and she spun. She recognized the voice, but an instant too late to stop her fist from slamming into his stomach.

He let out a very satisfying wheeze as he doubled over and she wasn't the least apologetic. She looked over to where a race bike, complete with cherry light on the handlebars, laid on its side in the grass.

"See what happens when they let you play with the toys? You just get in trouble."

He gave her a typical Cal grin as he straightened. "I deserved that. I just didn't think you spooked so easily."

Normally she didn't, but Megan wasn't about to tell him what had caused her spookiness. He would just laugh.

"Where did you get the bike?" she asked instead. "You're not a patrolman."

"Borrowed it from a friend. I can't drive my truck on the Esplanade."

He looked so…so heroic standing there with his hands on his hips. He wore tight spandex racing shorts and a very snug jersey, which only emphasized his muscular and very male body. She had to clear her throat before she could speak.

"What are you doing up at the crack of dawn?"

"Taking a day off. Thought I could talk you into going out on the boat with me."

"Boat?" The idea of floating around the bay with nothing to do but catch some sun was appealing. The thought of being on a boat with Cal was totally alluring. "Ah, I'm supposed to help Jeff."

Cal shook his head. "I talked to him last night. Mentioned the possibility of some investigative reporting for you, and since he knows that's your interest, he said he could get along without you."

"In other words, you lied…and to your brother, too."

"Naw." He stepped closer, his voice dropping to a rough whisper. "There's something that I really need you to

41

investigate." His dark eyes glittered with mischief and Megan couldn't help but smile.

"Did I ever tell you how much I like research?" She licked her lips for emphasis and was delighted when Cal groaned.

"You don't play fair," he growled.

"You started it."

"And I always finish what I start," he said as he straightened the bike and swing a long leg over the seat. "Pick you up in an hour. Dress warm as it'll be chilly on the water."

* * *

"You're going where; with who?" Stacy's voice rose an octave as Megan searched for some bottled water and snacks to put in a cooler.

"You heard me. Is there something wrong with the boat? Isn't it seaworthy?" She hoped to deflect the subject from what she feared was really on Stacy's mind. No such luck.

"The boat is awesome; a two sail schooner, and Cal is a first rate sailor. I was just wondering; well, it's really none of my business..."

"But you're going to ask anyway." Megan dumped a cluster of grapes into a plastic bag and added them to the cheese and crackers she'd already packed. "Never mind. I'll just tell you. Cal and I have been seeing each other for a little while."

Silence greeted her announcement, and she slowly turned to find Stacy braced against the counter, eyes wide and both hands covering her mouth.

Megan felt bad for not having told her best friend earlier, but this was just what she feared. What was she going to do if Stacy disapproved? She scrunched up her mouth, ready to apologize, when Stacy burst out laughing.

"This is too much! This is the best of all worlds! My very best friend and my very favorite brother...don't tell Jeff...he's my favorite in a different way. There's nothing I could have wished for that is this great!" She rushed over and hugged Megan until she couldn't breathe, which was a feat considering the difference in their sizes.

A horn sounded outside and Stacy took a step toward the door.

"Stacy, listen." Megan grabbed her arm. "It's all new and we're just sort of …exploring, and you know how your brother can get, so it's probably better not to say anything to him."

Stacy looked disappointed for a split second, then smiled again. "You are so right. He was always so secretive about who he was dating. But you have to know, Megan, he hasn't been seeing anyone for a really long time. He always said it was because of his job, but now..." She sighed. "Now, there's hope for him after all."

Megan kissed her cheek and grabbed the cooler. She only hoped that Stacy wouldn't be disappointed if things didn't work out. Hell, that went for her, too.

* * *

Cal didn't have to do any fast talking at all to get the day off when he called his chief. He never took days off, although his boss constantly bugged him about it. But that morning, when he had tracked Megan down, he realized he wanted to spend the day with her. Taking the boat out was a great excuse because they would be out of phone range. They could talk and…yeah, do all the things he thought about doing to her every waking minute when she wasn't in his sight.

"I brought a cooler," he said when she lifted a small red and white one into the truck bed.

"Mine has food."

He chuckled. "I guess I could have added some of that along with the beer."

"Uh-huh." She laughed, and he soon found that was the tone for the day.

She smiled with every instruction he gave her as they pushed off from the pier and he hoisted the first sail. She

43

laughed when the wind caught and they quickly skimmed the surface, and clapped her hands in delight when he unfurled the second sail and they fairly flew across the water. He headed toward Spectacle Island, well inside Boston Harbor. He had other things planned besides wrestling with the wind if they went out further and away from the protection of the numerous islands sheltering the bay.

"Come here," he called, motioning with his hand. She cautiously made her way to where he held the tiller, and when she would have sat beside him, he pulled her forward, sitting her snuggly in the curve of his spread legs, his arm tight around her waist.

He was in heaven when instead of stiffening, she instantly relaxed against his chest. Her hair blew across his face, and when she reached up to pull it back with a quick "sorry", he stopped further words with a hungry kiss. Despite the distraction of her hot response, Cal kept one eye peeled, then released her lips and adjusted the sails when the wind shifted.

"Nice," Megan said, and Cal wasn't sure if she referred to the kiss or the sailing, but it really didn't matter. He settled them back against the cushions and was content to let the wind take them where it would.

An hour later, he dropped sail and released the anchor in a shallow cove on the leeward side of Spectacle Island.

"Dad would sail us out here when we were kids and we'd snorkel all day." He looked out over the calm water, recalling the reckless and carefree days of his youth. Before life interfered.

"Why can't life be as simple nowadays?"

Megan carefully walked over to where he stood, circling his waist with her slim arms. He clasped a hand over her interlaced fingers. "Life does have a way of turning our lives around, or upside-down."

"Aw, man, I'm sorry, Megan." He turned in her arms. She had lost her parents when she was fourteen, and here he was whining about lost sailing days.

She put a finger to his lips. "It happened a long time ago." Her finger slid along his cheek and across his chin. "I'd rather concentrate on today." Little lines fanned out from her eyes as she smiled.

He covered that smile with one of his own, a kiss that swiftly went from sweet to savage as he ravaged her mouth, tongue flicking against hers, sharing her breath as he tugged her against him. Her curves fit him to perfection as she lifted her arms to circle his neck. Her breasts felt hot through the thin material of her shirt, and Cal wanted nothing more than to remove that barrier.

A wave hit the side of the boat and he grabbed the boom to keep them balanced as the boat rocked gently.

"Do you know why I brought you out here?" he asked as he brushed a strand of hair away from her face.

"To go snorkeling?"

He shook his head with a grin. "Too cold."

"Because you have no other friends?"

"Well, there is that." He frowned.

"I was teasing," she said quickly, but started laughing as he kissed her ear and nibbled her earlobe.

"I brought you out here so we wouldn't be interrupted by Stacy or Jeff."

"We could have gone to your place." Her breath was coming in short gasps as his hands slid under her shirt.

"They have keys." She was driving him crazy as her hands tunneled through his hair, her fingers tickling his neck. He took her mouth in another desperate kiss, his hands starting a slow slide up her belly.

"Help!"

The cry had Cal jerking around, instincts instantly on alert. A small Sunfisher was rapidly approaching, apparently out of control. One of the people on board was frantically waving while the other jerked on the line.

"Drop your sail!" Call yelled as he quickly grabbed the gaff. The boat, although small, was on a direct collision course with them.

"Flip the bumpers over the side," he called to Megan as he kept a steady eye on the other boat. He would have to

45

catch the front of the small boat just right to flip it around and bring it up against their boat, instead of getting rammed. And he had to do it without capsizing the smaller craft.

"Drop your damned sail!" He hollered again and then it was too late. Even though he was braced, when the gaff caught the front nose of the Sunfisher, the force of the hit threw him back a few steps. He felt Megan behind him, lending her weight to his.

The instant the back end swung around and bounced against the bumpers, Megan was there grabbing the edge of the boat to keep it steady.

The sail of the smaller boat was still taut to the wind, causing it to push against his larger schooner. Cal could hear his anchor dragging against the bottom of the shallow cove.

"Drop the—"

"It's stuck," the older of the two boys interrupted, even as he jerked on the line.

"Get over here," Cal ordered, wrapping the boat's head line around a cleat on his.

As soon as the two boys scrambled aboard, he lithely stepped over onto the Sunfisher. With a swift jerk on the line, the sail dropped, letting the boat now rock gently against the side of his own. He examined the pulleys and found one bent just enough to catch the line when it was supposed to release the sail.

Climbing back over the rail, he skewered the boys with a dark look. "What the hell are you doing out this far if you can't sail a damned boat?"

"Cal," Megan said his name softly, trying to placate but he ignored her.

"You've got no damned reason to be out here…" He broke off when the younger boy started to cry. He couldn't be any older than Jeff had been the first time their father had taken them sailing.

With a sigh, he rubbed a hand over his face, trying to get his emotions under control. It was Cal's nature to protect. It was the most basic reason he had become a

46

policeman. Dropping down on a seat, he watched as Megan calmly gave the boys bottles of water and wrapped them each in a towel.

"What're your names?" he finally asked.

"J-jer-Jeremy Sl-ater," the older one stammered, his shoulders shaking. "This is my brother, Joey." The younger one looked up at Cal from beneath his lashes.

"You certified?"

"Yes. Yes, sir," the youth answered.

"Well, at least you had life vests on. It's too damned early in the season to be swimming in the bay regardless."

"Yes sir." The boy nodded as he agreed, still shaking.

"What would you have done—?"

"Cal."

The one word stopped his tirade. He looked up to where Megan hovered over the boys, a hand on each of their shoulders.

"The rope was stuck," she said. "I'm just glad we were here to help, so let's get these two back to the harbor. Okay?"

The fact that she added that little question at the end didn't fool him. She was ordering him around. He hung his head in defeat. All his carefully laid plans to seduce her were down the drain. For now, he would accept it, but there would come a time when he would be in charge and she would not be sidestepping his advances.

Chapter 5

The next time Cal stopped at the B&B, his sister bombarded him with questions, surprisingly not of a personal nature.

"Do you know what's wrong with Megan? She won't talk about it, but I just know something's up. She's burning the midnight oil writing stories for any of the papers who will give her a lead. She's doing three of Jeff's tours downtown but she refuses to do the tour to the river and it's been really successful an--"

"Slow down." Cal held up both hands to ward off the onslaught. When his sister got on a tear, she barely came up for breath. "Why would I know what's up?"

"Because you're dating, that's why. And I know you. You interrogate your dates like they were wanted for some crime."

"I do not," he reacted immediately. At least he didn't think he did. He'd have to think about that later. Now, Stacy's worry about Megan became his worry.

"She's doing the downtown tours – Paul Revere and the cemetery?" He knew how she felt about history, and wondered why she would suddenly throw herself totally into Jeff's business, except for the night tour. He recalled what she had asked about the house and its peculiarities, but shrugged it off. Megan was too smart to believe in ghosts.

"Where is she now?" Although he didn't think he interrogated his friends, he intended to find out what was up with Megan.

Stacy glanced at the clock on the wall. "She should be finishing a tour by half past. I don't know where."

Cal headed for the back door, his sister's words ringing in his ears.

"I'm glad you're dating Megan, but if you hurt her, I'll kill you."

She didn't mean it, he thought as he climbed into his truck. At least he didn't think she did.

Cal had just started the engine when his cell rang. "Garrett."

"Sorry to disturb you on your day off," his boss's voice boomed. "The sheriff from Porchello called and asked for help, and I figured it was right up your alley so you might as well look into it."

"Hell, Bob, did you hear yourself? D...a...y...o...f...f." He spelled the word.

"But you never really take days off," his boss replied. "You lose vacation days every year."

He was right. In all his years with the police department, Cal had rarely taken any time off. That was before Megan. Now he was using his vacation as often as he could.

"Cal, you there?"

He corralled his thoughts. "What is it that can't wait?"

"A dead body."

Shit. He pulled out of the parking lot and stepped on the gas.

"I'll get there as soon as I can." He punched the phone off then immediately dialed Megan's number, getting her location and telling her he would pick her up in ten minutes.

Taking Megan with him was good for a number of reasons. He would have time to find out what was going on with her, even if it was at a crime scene. But more important, before she became an investigative reporter, she had worked for a crime scene unit. He was extremely good at reading people and hearing the lies behind alibis, but she had skills well beyond those of most police officers, and an intuitiveness that lent itself well to solving crimes.

"Why did you pick me up?" she asked as she climbed into the cab. "I'd have been home in less than an hour." She

49

was dressed in jeans and a casual shirt and she tossed a bag in the back that Cal assumed was her tour costume.

He turned back onto the highway that led west out of town.

"There's been an accident in Porchello that the chief wants me to look into. These small towns often only have one cop – usually a retired guy who wants to draw a paycheck but really not have to do much work. Porchello doesn't get much crime, even in the height of tourist season, which is now."

"An accident?" She glanced at him and he could see the question in her gaze. "As in vehicle, house fire? You're a detective, not a traffic cop or arson investigator."

He easily recalled what he had thought about her insight. "Dead body."

"Oh." She glanced out the window then back. "But why take me?"

He wasn't sure he wanted to tell her he missed her, or get into the emotion of wanting her with him night and day, so he settled on the familiar.

"You want to do investigative reporting. I'm just giving you a chance to see if there's a story to be had."

They made good time to Porchello and soon were cruising along the main street that ran in front of the resorts with their fake chalet frontages.

"When something like this happens, the local authorities usually call the nearest big city for help. Unfortunately, my boss then called me."

Pedestrians paid little heed to the cars as they trekked diagonally across the street to get to whatever was of interest on the other side. He swore as he slammed on the brakes. "Can't they see the freaking flashing lights?"

Meg twisted her long auburn hair in a knot and shot him a grin. "You are not a patient man, are you, Garrett?"

He found the address he needed and swerved to the curb, punching the flashers and turning off the truck.

"I just don't know what McGuire's thinking, offering my services," he grumbled over the situation. "Most times he steers clear of getting involved in another town's situations."

""But you said when small towns don't have the man power, BPD helps out. And in this case, we're talking about a death. That's probably not the usual crime for a town like Porchello."

He got out and came around to her side as she jumped down. "I know, but--"

"You can't park here, mister. Can't you see it's cordoned off?"

Cal flipped his badge at the man in washed-out khaki and kept walking, Megan right on his heels. "Who's in charge?" he questioned, clearly implying that khaki-man wasn't.

"I am." Another man approached, this one not much better. He was short, extremely thin and had a nervous twitch. He tugged off a glove as he extended his hand. "Barney."

That's who he reminds me of, Cal thought. "Barney Fife?" He shook the man's hand. Barney apparently didn't appreciate his humor.

"Sheriff Lucas Barney. And you would be?" He took a quick step sideways when Megan tried to duck under the yellow tape.

Cal gave a mental groan. He knew damned good and well the sheriff had seen his badge. Besides, he had been the one to call for help. "Detective Cal Garrett, BPD, and this is Megan Anderson." He deliberately left off any title, hoping they'd assume she was also with BPD.

"You sure got here fast." The small town sheriff sounded like he regretted his call to Cal's supervisor.

Well, hell. Cal hated murder, loved his job, and would do anything in his power to put the bad guys behind bars. But he usually had the backing of the people he worked with. He hoped he wouldn't have to stay long, and wouldn't be called on further than this first step. Suppressing his temper, he gave a curt, "What's up?"

"We have a dead body," Khaki-man said.

51

No shit, Cal thought, walking past the two and squatting next to Megan, who had scooted around the officials and was examining the body. It was by a resort pool, laying half on the sidewalk, the upper body hidden in some shrubbery.

"Please tell me he died of some natural cause so we can get out of here," he whispered.

She shook her head. "I'm no medical examiner, but it just might be more than that."

"Like?"

"Murder." Her tone was hushed, but it didn't keep Barney from jumping into it.

"We don't have murders in Porchello. And who did you say you were?"

Cal stood, towering over the sheriff by a good foot. "She's with me. That's all you need to know." He glanced sideways to where two EMTs stood, hands in pockets, waiting. "Do you have a medical examiner?"

"No."

"Who determines cause of death?"

The sheriff jutted out his chest. "I do and I'm saying this was an accident."

"Then why did you call BPD?"

"He's from Boston," the deputy answered. "John Dough."

"He's a John Doe but you know he's from Boston?" Cal could feel the headache start right behind his right eye. He pressed the heel of his hand to his forehead.

The deputy seemed to enjoy Cal's confusion, smirking slightly as he held a wallet out to the sheriff. Cal snatched it away.

Sure enough, the guy's name was Dough, age twenty-two.

"Sheriff." Megan addressed the local authority when she came to stand beside Cal, but she put her hand lightly on his back, rubbing in a circle. He narrowed his gaze when she glanced his way, knowing she was telling him to keep it together. "There appears to be blunt force trauma to the

52

back of this young man's head, and some bruising around the neck, which might indicate he was strangled."

"And just exactly who are you again?" The sheriff glanced over at the body and back to her.

"Megan Anderson, from Boston." She smiled, extending her hand.

Megan's smile could light up a room and bring a man to his knees. It had the desired effect on Barney. He stammered and flushed and completely forgot to ask her for further credentials.

"Well, now, I suppose I could call the coroner from Patterson, the next county over."

"You do that, Sheriff. Then call BPD and let them know." Cal grabbed Megan's hand and turned to walk back to his vehicle.

"Where will you be? I'll need to call you," the sheriff hollered after him.

"On vacation. I don't have a phone."

He saw Megan giggle as she settled into the passenger seat and he had to work on keeping a straight face as he rounded the front of the truck.

"Then how'd you know to come—" The sheriff's question was cut off when Cal started the truck and raced the engine. He saw the deputy point in his direction and say something, to which the sheriff nodded, then shrugged. He could only imagine they were discussing his ancestry.

* * *

Cal's cell phone buzzed just as they pulled into the parking at a condo complex, but he ignored it. Megan raised a brow in question.

"My place," he said as he shut off the truck. "Thought I could at least fix you dinner for ruining what was left of your day."

"You didn't ruin anything," she said as they walked up the steps. "It was fun."

"Investigating a possible murder?" He pushed the door open and gestured for her to precede him.

His condo was ultra modern and very male in that the furniture was leather and the coffee table, chairs, and accessories were chrome and glass. What surprised her was that it was impeccably neat. She turned as she heard his keys drop into a dish on a table by the door, and watched as he pulled his gun and holster from his back and carefully set it in the drawer of the table.

"The chance to do something different," she replied to his question, then added, "You didn't take much time with the poor sheriff."

"For Christ's sake, Meg, he's Barney from Mayberry."

She *tsked* and shook her head as she slowly rounded the couch. "It's Lucas Barney, not Barney Fife."

"Regardless, he called, we answered, although he apparently didn't like what we had to say." He grabbed her wrist when she would have sat down on the couch and tugged her closer. "Besides, there's not a damned thing we can do until they autopsy. Natural causes and we're totally out of it. Murder and McGuire will have to assign someone if the sheriff wants the help."

He twined his fingers with hers and wrapped his arms around her waist, effectively pinning her arms behind her back and her chest to his.

Megan wasn't sure how she was managing a coherent thought. "I'm pretty sure it wasn't natural causes. There was nothing close for him to fall against and hit his head – no trees, no cement benches – nothing."

"You are brilliantly correct." He nibbled the lobe of her ear, then kissed a path down her throat. She shivered in awareness. "Now, here's a clue." He rubbed his hips against hers. "Can you guess what's going to happen next?"

"You are so crass. It certainly doesn't take a forensic expert to figure you out."

"Does that bother you?" He didn't give her time to answer but took her mouth in a fiery kiss. He still had her hands pinned so she couldn't touch him like she wanted, but answered his kiss with some heat of her own.

He backed off first and when she looked, his gaze was narrow but hot.

"Like it?" she asked, letting her voice drop to a sexy rumble.

"Like an addict loves his dealer."

His phone vibrated against his waist where it was clipped to his belt. He jerked it off, looked at the read-out and gave a colorful oath. He let her go and answered it.

Megan could tell by the tone of his voice that Cal wasn't happy with whoever he was talking to, but there wasn't much she could do about it. Cal would tell her what was going on when he was ready.

It was funny how things worked out. Just like Cal, she had once had a job that demanded a lot of time and energy, and if not secrecy, at least a high level of discretion. If any of her stories had leaked before she had completed her investigation, not only might the culprits not get caught, but another newspaper or magazine could have scooped her and she wouldn't have been able to sell her story. With Cal, he couldn't speak his suspicions during a case. The DA would have his job if a leak occurred that allowed a defense attorney to claim improper handling of a case.

Up until now, Cal hadn't really talked about his job and all the nitty-gritty that went with it. Instead, they had kept their conversations general as they had learned about each other on a personal level.

She knew Cal would talk to her when and if he could. The fact that he had taken her with him to Porchello just proved her point.

But sometimes she couldn't wait. She grabbed his hand when he shut off the phone. "Cal, what's up?"

He made a face. "Stac stopped by earlier with Tortellini Alfredo. It should be in the oven. You want to make a salad while I shower?"

She squeezed his hand then let go. "Sure. Do you have any wine to go with it?"

"I'm going to need something stronger than that," he muttered as he walked away.

* * *

"Talk to me, Garrett," Megan said as soon as he pushed his plate back.

Cal gave a frustrated sigh. Among all the other things he liked about Megan was her intuitiveness, although it didn't take much tonight for her to know he was pissed.

"My boss called. Even though the report isn't complete on John Dough, they're calling it a suspicious death and treating it as a homicide."

"Like we didn't already know that."

"Yeah, well, he also said I apparently pissed off the local authorities. Barney told him I was arrogant, pushy and generally overstepped my authority."

Meg smiled. "Like we didn't already know that."

He scowled at her but knew she was right. He had little patience for incompetence. "Even so, McGuire has offered my services. He said the department needed to stay involved since the kid was from Boston."

"And?"

He sighed. "And the kid's old man is on the city commission."

"Ah. That's what really gets you, doesn't it?"

"It's bad enough that he has me investigating with some Podunk cop shop, but he knows I hate being pressured by politics." He scooted back his chair and collected their plates, walking into the kitchen area. "I'll have to get you home and then figure out how quickly I can get this wrapped up."

"No way." She followed him into the kitchen where she ran some water into the sink.

He wrapped his arms around her waist while she washed their few dishes. "I thought you had tours to do; history to recreate."

She threw a raspberry over her shoulder. "Jeff will have to get along without me. He knows I'm still looking for reporter work. Besides, all I have to do is make a few calls and I'll have this story sold."

Cal doubted this case would see the light of day in the news because of who the kid was. He also wondered if it might not be better for Megan to do the tour thing so he could concentrate on the case. He wrapped her tighter in his embrace. Then again, there were definitely advantages to having her here. He bumped her with his hips.

"That's the only reason?"

She turned, looping her sudsy hands around his neck. "That, and I figured I could protect you from the sun-seeking, bikini-clad babes who seem to be all over Porchello."

"They've got nothing on you, babe," he growled as he lightly nipped her neck.

"Oh, then you did notice them hovering all over the crime scene?"

He laughed. "I'd have to be dead not to. That doesn't mean anything." He lifted his head to meet her gaze. "I'm a one woman man." Before she could make some snappy comeback, he sealed her mouth with his.

The kiss sizzled as it always did and he had to wonder if they would burn themselves out. Before he let things get out of hand, he lifted his head.

"Go sit down. I'll bring us another drink."

When he entered the living room just minutes later, he found Megan curled up on the couch sound asleep. He put the drinks aside and sat on the coffee table facing her. He gently brushed her hair back, caressing her soft cheek.

"Hey, sweetie."

She rolled her head from side to side, murmuring something about shadows and ghosts and green haze.

Cal shook her a little harder. "The late nights are catching up with you."

"I haven't been sleeping well," she mumbled as she sat up. "Maybe I should sleep here?"

Cal grew instantly hard. "You wouldn't get any sleep here either." His gaze grew steamy. "Are you ready for that?"

He saw the indecision in her eyes and knew it wasn't a fair question when she was half asleep. With a sigh he stood and put out a hand.

"Come on. It's time to take you home."

Chapter 6

Cal's phone buzzed early the next morning. The number was unfamiliar, but had a local prefix and his gut said he'd have the number memorized before long.

"Sheriff Barney here. We've got a situation."

God, he sounded just like the TV script. "Just give me the facts."

"Seems our boy was involved in some pretty heavy stuff. Get down here, pronto."

Pretty heavy stuff? What the fuck did that mean?

"Sheriff, my boss generously volunteered my assistance when you called the first time. That does not mean I have to continue on your case, and it sure as shit doesn't mean you get to order me around."

When the sheriff refused to shut up, Cal grudgingly agreed to go out to Porchello and visit with the characters Barney kept insisting were reliable witnesses.

He immediately called Megan. "Can you be ready to roll in half an hour?"

"Where?" She sounded groggy and Cal felt sorry for waking her up, especially when she had said she wasn't getting much sleep.

"Mayberry."

"Oh, Cal, I can't."

"It's a story." He tried to bribe her.

"It may be," she replied, "but I promised Jeff to do Jamie's tours today. The kid is working two jobs and going to school, and he has finals today."

"Jeff?"

"You know better," she said and he could tell she was fully awake now. "Please don't give me a hard time."

Cal knew she needed the money and he was tempted to tell her that he would take care of her. However, he was smart enough to know that was not something a twenty-first century woman wanted to hear. Besides, it also meant fast-forwarding their relationship in a direction he wasn't sure she was ready to go.

"Thomas Rock, Richard Bier, and Harold Breeze." Sheriff Barney pointed to the three kids seated along a bench in the police station when Cal arrived.

"Tom, Dick and Harry? Are you kidding me?" Cal quipped.

The red-headed young man stood. "That's Harold, sir." He stuck out his hand and Cal shook it. The kid, probably in his twenties, had a strong grip and it implied that Cal should indeed call him Harold.

"Okay." He gave a curt nod before turning back to the sheriff. "Where can I take these three to talk?"

"We can use my office," Barney said.

Cal shook his head. "You've already talked; they've talked. Now it's my turn to see what they have to say." When the sheriff looked like he would argue, Cal added, "It's your case, but it's sometimes better to get a different perspective." Christ, he hated politics and kissing ass.

Cal was somewhat surprised to see the sheriff's office. It was spacious, and unlike most law enforcement facilities, this one contained oak furniture, tall wood bookcases and a square, glass-topped coffee table. A sofa sat on one side and two identical, high-backed leather chairs on the other. He motioned the boys to the sofa.

"My name is Cal Garrett, and I'm with the Boston Police Department. Sheriff Barney (he almost added Fife) has asked me to look into the death of John Dough." He refrained from saying *murder* in case they either didn't know or were hiding something. Either way, the element of surprise could be useful.

"Who wants to start telling me what's going on?" His gaze scanned the three, none of whom looked uncomfortable or guilty.

60

"It's just a game; a computer simulation," said the brown haired guy.

"You are?"

"Thomas Rock, from New York."

Cal looked at the blonde youth. "Then you must be Dick."

The kid grimaced and Cal didn't blame him. Who would name their kid anything that could be shortened to a body part?

"Richard Bier, from Philadelphia."

Cal looked at Harold. "Where are you from?"

"LA."

"How the hell did Philly, New York, L. A. and Boston end up in Porchello? Did you all know each other before you came here?"

"Only on line," Tom replied.

Cal had a fleeting wish for Megan, who loved what she called cybercrime. He hoped he wasn't dealing with that.

"What's this computer game?"

"Your Money or Your Life," Harold quickly said, and Cal got the impression he was the leader of this pack of computer nerds.

"Well, that sounds like a good murder and mayhem game to play on a weekend," Cal sarcastically replied.

"No, you don't understand. It's all about building fortresses and hidden treasure, not about murder and violence."

So they knew. "Someone's dead."

"It's not supposed to be that way."

"Why didn't you come forward as soon as it happened?"

Richard answered this time. "We heard there had been an accident here and someone died. We don't know each other's real names in the game, but when a particular avatar didn't appear on line for over a day, we thought, well, that someone was playing some kind of trick to throw us off balance."

"So you don't know for sure John's the adventurer?"

"Its avatar," Harold boldly corrected him.

61

Avatar? Now Cal knew he should have insisted Megan come with him. He used the computer about as often as he went skiing in the Alps. "Let's start at the beginning."

"We're testing this computer game for the creator, before it's released to the public."

"How many is *we*?" Cal asked.

"I don't know," Harold replied. "Everyone's on-line at different times and some may have more than one avatar. It's hard to tell."

"Who is the creator?"

They all shrugged. "We don't know that either. He just goes by Simon, and we follow the instructions in his emails."

"Like *Simon Says*?" Cal raised a brow, wondering if he had fallen into some time warp. "Okay, then how did he find you?"

Harold again answered. "Through gaming blogs, Facebook, Twitter. You know."

Cal didn't know. He used the computer for work only, and even then preferred good old fashioned investigation and hard-ball questioning.

"Explain the game to me."

The boys exchanged looks. "Are you familiar with *Monopoly*?" asked Tom.

Cal scowled at them. He wasn't senile.

"Think of it as a cross between *Monopoly* and *Survivor* with *Minecraft* components, played on the internet. People buy and sell imaginary artifacts, make alliances, double cross and hide from each other, and the ultimate winner is the one with everything."

"Sounds like Wall Street or the banking system."

"It's just a game," said Tom. "We only signed up to test the simulation. No one was supposed to get hurt."

"Well, that didn't happen, did it?" Cal grumbled. "How do I get in touch with this Simon guy?"

They looked at each other then back at him. Dick answered. "We only get messages from him. It's a 'no-reply' email address."

"There must be some way to talk to him. What if there's a glitch in the game?" Cal asked. "Or a player gets murdered?" He narrowed his gaze at each, hoping to catch a reaction but there was nothing.

"It's only speculation," Harold said hesitantly, "but…"

"What?"

"Simon has to be monitoring the game since he always seems to know if someone hits a glitch in the program, even before it's posted."

"And?" Cal felt like he was playing *Twenty Questions* and was getting a little short on patience.

"Since John, if that's whose avatar is missing, is no longer playing, maybe something will appear on the game message board about it," Tom said.

"How long is this game supposed to last?"

"Until winner takes all," replied Tom.

"And you three are here for the duration? What about the other players? Is everyone here in Porchello?"

Dick shook his head. "I doubt it, although some may be and we just don't know it."

"Then how did you three land here?"

"We've been gaming against each other before," said Harold, "and when this came up, we decided to all come here for spring break, meet, and work on the simulation together."

Cal rubbed a hand over his eyes. "Okay. This is what's going to happen." He handed each of them his card. "If anyone hears *anything*," he emphasized the word, "you call me. If anything out of the ordinary happens, you call."

"Ah." Dick looked like he was half afraid to speak.

Cal gave a sigh. Patience, he reminded himself.

"We're playing a simulation that we've never played before and everything is new. How are we going to know if something is out of the ordinary?"

Good question, thought Cal. Again he wished for Megan, who would probably have an answer. All he could think to say was, "You'll know."

* * *

63

"Jeff has laryngitis and there is a full tour of twenty-five people tonight," Stacy wailed at Megan the minute she came out of the bathroom.

Megan slammed a hand against her chest. "Good night, you scared me to death!" She pulled the towel off her hair and it immediately fell across her face. She brushed it out of her eyes. Stacy was sitting cross-legged on her bed, apparently lying in wait. Megan had stood extra long in the shower, letting the hot water sooth her tired muscles after a restless night's sleep.

She was jerked back into the present by her friend. "Meg?"

"So, give everyone a cup of tea when they arrive and a rain-check." Megan picked up her brush and started on the tangles in her long hair. She seriously thought about cutting it short, but Cal seemed to like running his fingers through it and she easily recalled how sensuous that felt.

"Megan, we can't do that. Jeff texted that this will be the biggest group yet. Besides, it's a relatively new tour and word will get around that we're not reliable."

Megan heard the emphasis on the word *we*, and realized that even though it was Jeff's business, Stacy was directly linked by virtue of the house.

"Get Toni to narrate."

"She can't. She's Laurie."

"Matthew?" Megan tossed out, knowing Matt had been at the house almost every night there had been a tour, even though Jeff didn't need him to critique anymore. She didn't know if it was the history, the legend, or Stacy that brought him.

Stacy was shaking her head. "He's working at something or the other and can't get away."

Megan didn't know exactly what Matt did, and Stacy had never said, but he seemed to have a lot of free time on his hands. When Stacy didn't say anything else, Megan flipped her hair back and looked at her friend.

"No," she sputtered at the look in Stacy's eyes.

"You have to." It was practically a wail.

"Maybe I have plans, too," Megan protested weakly. She hadn't heard from Cal since he had dropped her off last night, but hoped against hope that he would call and give her a reprieve. She picked up her phone from where it lay on her bedside table and looked. No messages; no voice mail.

"I already called Cal."

"You what?" Megan's voice rose.

Stacy's head scrunched into her shoulders. "He said he was headed out of town and probably wouldn't be back till late."

Wait until the next time I see him, thought Megan. So much for any legitimate excuse.

"Stacy, can't you do it?"

Even as she asked, Stacy was shaking her head. "I don't know all the lines. I only know Mrs. McCluer and the beginning that takes place at the house." Her huge, pleading gaze locked with Megan's. "Please?"

Megan sighed deeply, shaking her head even as she reluctantly agreed. "Alright, but if you see your brother, tell him he owes me big time."

Stacy bounced off the bed with a squeal and hugged Megan tightly. "Thank you, thank you." She raced for the door. "I need to make scones." Then she stopped and turned. "Which one owes you?"

Megan narrowed her gaze, thinking of Cal going off without her and Jeff pleading illness. "Both of them."

Chapter 7

Megan knew the script even though she had only done the *River's Edge* tour once. Still, she read through it again that afternoon. Being part of the group when Jeff discussed the different narrative and action parts, and being his 'apprentice' was not the only reason she knew the story.

She dreamed of Laurie McCluer. She heard voices in the night and echoes of that long-ago happening along the Charles River. Not that she wanted to. She even took a sleep aid some nights, but the dreams still came and she always remembered them in the morning. But she seemed to be the only one who had the dreams and heard the voices. Casual questioning of Stacy and Jeff, as she had done with Cal, proved that. Add that to the fact she had been the only one to see that green haze the first time she'd done the tour.

She thought maybe she was projecting herself into the legend. Just last night, she had dreamed she was Laurie, walking along the riverbank, arm in arm with Logan Mallory, her betrothed. But when she looked up at him, he was the spitting image of Cal. At that point, she had awakened with a gasp.

Crazy thoughts came and went as she pinned up her hair and covered it with a snood. Why was Cal in her dreams? She could only think her inner self had Logan looking like him because Cal was of a similar nature, wanting justice and striving to care for those close to him. And perhaps because she wanted him to be to her what Logan had been to Laurie.

She laid the script aside. She knew it was only a story handed down through the generations. So why did she think there was more to it than some legend?

Most legends were based on historical facts of one kind or the other. And of all the cities on the eastern seaboard, Boston was often proclaimed as the most historic and therefore could be said to have the most legends, ghosts, and other lore. Well, there was Salem and the witch trials, and she was suddenly very happy she wasn't doing reenactments there.

Regardless, it certainly enhanced a building's allure to have a ghost or hints of buried treasure attached to it. In the case of the McCluer's, the fact he was a tea merchant around the time of the Revolutionary War certainly made for a good story since importing tea from Britain was one of the great controversies of the time. After all, Boston was home of the renowned Boston Tea Party.

Megan buttoned up the front of her bodice and scrutinized herself in the mirror. Here she was, the last person in the world to be reenacting history, getting ready to enthrall tourists. Well, it was what made the world go round, she thought as she climbed the stairs from the basement apartment. And it was money in her pocket.

Money or not, she almost changed her mind about doing the tour when she looked out the back windows. Fog had rolled in, shrouding the area in a gray mist. There was supposed to be a half moon, but all it managed to do was cast an eerie glow. Megan couldn't help but think about the story and the fact that Laurie had disappeared on a foggy night – just like this one.

"Maybe we should cancel, after all," she said to Stacy upon entering the kitchen.

"No, no. This is actually great," her friend replied. "Fog just enhances the mystery of it all. Besides, we already have a room full of anxious tourists." She lifted the tea service. "Grab that plate of scones, will you?"

Megan cast a last, furtive glance toward the window, knowing there was no help for it. She just hoped the *real* ghost of Laurie McCluer would not make an appearance while she was on duty.

* * *

Cal drove back into town in the fog. There was never a rhyme or reason as to when the fog rolled in through the bay. He knew it had to do with barometric pressure and temperature and humidity and all that, but it wasn't something the normal person would really anticipate. All he did know was that often times, fog brought out the weirdoes, just like a full moon. Thankfully he wasn't a beat cop anymore.

He slowed his speed, flipped on his fog lights, and crept along with the rest of the traffic. He knew the town well enough that he never missed a turn as he maneuvered the streets towards the Blue Rose B&B, hoping to catch Megan and question her about the story Tom, Dick and Harry had told him. It seemed suspicious that anyone would travel all the way across the country just to play a computer game, but none of the boys appeared the least guilty. And Cal was very good at reading faces and body language, even if he wasn't that good at computer crap.

The small amount of parking behind the B&B, as well as along the side street, was packed and he ended up parking several blocks away. He really didn't mind walking in the fog, he thought, remembering the countless times in his youth when he and Jeff would use the fog to help them hide behind trees and shrubs and scare people passing by. It was a wonder they didn't end up in juvey for some of their exploits.

He took the steps two at a time and let himself in the front door. The lights had been dimmed and for a change, the sitting room was empty. Strange, even for a weekday, given it was high tourist season.

"Hello?" His query echoed off the mahogany walls.

"Back here."

Pushing open the kitchen door he found only Stacy, dressed in her costume, loading the dishwasher with tea cups and saucers.

"Tour tonight?" He opened the fridge and grabbed a beer, rewarding himself for having suffered through the Mayberry ordeal.

"I think Jeff could schedule them every night if he had enough people to do them. We had over twenty-five participants tonight, which would have been great except Jeff has laryngitis and couldn't narrate."

"Well who's doing it then?" He gave a sigh as the cold beer slid down his throat.

"Megan."

He spewed out the second swallow. "What?"

"It took some finagling but she finally agreed."

"Well, *damn*." He had wanted to talk to her about the case, although that wasn't the only reason he wanted to see her.

Stacy turned toward him. "She really didn't want to do it. I don't understand. She does the downtown tours, but for some reason she doesn't like to do *To the River's Edge*. Any ideas, Mr. Detective?"

Cal shrugged. Apparently Megan hadn't said anything to Stacy about her feelings where the house was concerned so he decided not to bring it up. While he didn't believe in ghosts, girls were different and he couldn't see spooking his sister. Especially when she was home alone.

"My expertise is murder and mayhem, not ghostly tours. So how long have they been gone?"

"Just thirty minutes or so. They should be on the Charles Street walk-over to the Esplanade about now."

Cal didn't want to interrupt the tour and since Megan wouldn't be able to talk to him anyway, he figured he would just go to the Pub and meet them at the end. He gave his sister a brotherly pat on the top of her dust mop cap, tossed his empty into the recycle bin, and left by the back door.

* * *

Megan's tour group had stopped at the edge of the Esplanade near Charles Street, clustering close together in the fog even though they were virtual strangers. Her nerves had been all right so far. She had recited the background

69

and built the story up while leading the group around several blocks and down a dark alley.

Now, when the small group of re-enactors, previously hidden by the fog, lit their candle lanterns and walked across the grass toward the large oak tree, she felt a shiver down her back and her lantern shook as she held it aloft.

"The small group of friends," she began but then had to pause, hoping the quiver would leave her voice. She saw a few of the women tourists step closer to their companions and imagined they thought the quiver was part of the story line. She knew better, and the shivery feelings, like icy fingers down her spine, didn't help.

She started again, her voice still breathy. *"The small group of friends sat beneath the huge oak by the bank of the Charles River and felt relatively safe. Thinking no British ship or soldiers would venture this far, they could speak in relative freedom. They were not the Sons of Liberty. They were young and some of them female, so they did not quite understand their place as the hands of destiny tugged their hearts and minds in different directions."*

Megan's voice dropped to a mysterious whisper. *"It is said of this night, though, that their arguments for forcing the British soldiers to leave their beloved Boston were quite adamant, and that Logan Mallory's voice rose loud and clear above the rest."* She set her lantern on the ground and covered it with the black cloth she carried. This shrouded the area further and focused the audience's attention on the small group in front of them.

"We must not allow them to tell us how to live our lives!" Re-enactor Logan Mallory proclaimed, a clinched fist against his heart. "I, for one, am most willing to give my life for the freedoms we have."

All the others *on stage* cheered his courage and loudly admired his spirit, raising their hands to his in a show of unity.

Megan's heart pounded as the group of re-enactors departed, leaving the young Logan and Laurie alone in a small circle of lantern light. Even though she knew it was just a play, and that it was really Toni and not Laurie there by the tree, she felt the inexorable urge to rush forward and grab her to prevent her disappearance. When one of the other tour guide assistants cleared his throat, Megan remembered the script.

"Laurie could not have known the danger that lurked just around the bend in the river," she said in a soft voice. *"For as secretive as they thought their meetings were, someone had betrayed them."*

The actors' lantern was doused and Toni's scream pierced the night. The reaction of the crowd was immediate. Gasps of surprise, and perhaps a little fear; nervous laughter, even a muttered "What the hell?" All signs of a very successful historical tour.

But as Toni's scream faded into the fog, Megan heard whispers just off to her right, whereas the tourists all stood to the left.

"It's time," the softly accented murmur drifted across her awareness. "You can help me." She felt a tug on the sleeve of her dress, then an icy cold touch on her cheek.

She quickly flipped the cloth off her lantern and glanced all around but nothing, at least not what she could see, was out of place. There was no one there who shouldn't be. She looked back toward the tree, its shadow barely visible through the fog. Toni and the Logan guy (she couldn't remember his name) weren't supposed to light their lanterns again as they disappeared, but she could detect a pinpoint of light moving along the walk.

A hazy, green shape separated from the two and darted back to the large oak tree, disappearing behind it.

"Did you see that?" she asked no one in particular.

"What?"

"Where?" The questions leaped at her from the group. Realizing she had been daydreaming and they were getting restless, she hastily began the narrative again.

"There was much speculation as to why Laurie was taken, and by whom, and it is unfortunate that no one had the courage to investigate until the mystery was solved." As she spoke, she slowly walked backwards along the running path at the edge of the Esplanade, knowing the tour

group would follow. "If you will follow me to O'Brien's Pub, we'll conclude the story in much the same way that we think it was originally told."

* * *

Cal was getting impatient and for the third time, asked the bartender if he was sure the tour group was coming in.

"Far as I know. Haven't heard otherwise." His disgruntled reply only made Cal edgier, but no sooner had he spoken then the front door opened and in spilled a large group of people, all chattering and laughing. Some, apparently quite anxious for a refreshment after the walk from the park, came right to the bar to order, while most settled themselves at the small round tables in groups.

As an observer of human nature, Cal watched as they paired off or hesitated to one side while waiting to see who sat where. He could tell which ones were related, which were traveling together, and which ones were like strangers stuck in an elevator together – instant friends for the duration, but not bosom buddies for life. But he didn't see Megan.

"Hey." He stepped over as one of the people, dressed in old fashioned attire, set a lantern on the bar. "Where's Megan?"

He looked around in surprise. "I don't know. She was with us all the way." He paused. "I thought, but the fog's so bad, I can't be sure."

Cal looked toward the door then back at the guide. "Can you do the rest of the program?"

The kid made a face, started to shake his head, then slowly nodded. Cal was sure the expression on his own face had persuaded the guy. "Sure, I guess. Not much left anyway."

Cal left quickly. Something wasn't right. First, Megan does a tour she doesn't like to do, then she disappears? It sounded too much like the original story, but Cal Garrett was not a man who believed in legends and ghosts.

He backtracked the tour, knowing from Jeff the streets they traversed between the park and the pub. It was hard to see in the fog but he did run into a few folks out for a stroll. Even on a bad weather night, Boston was alive with people, but none of them wore an eighteenth century dress and bonnet.

He trotted down the sidewalk, then turned to cut across the grass toward the river and he almost missed her. Sound was amplified in the heavy air and just the scrape of a shoe sounded like thunder. He swerved to the left and stopped when he saw the shadow huddled on a park bench.

"What are you doing?" he asked softly as he approached. She was staring down at her hands, clasped together in her lap. She didn't move; didn't even seem to have heard him and he didn't want to frighten her.

"Megan?" He took a step closer.

She gave a squawk and her head flew up, looking left then right. The instant she saw him she jumped up and flung herself at him. Cal stumbled backward but managed to keep them both upright.

"It's all right, baby," he cooed as she shook in his arms. "You're all right." He led her back to the bench and sat, pulling her onto his lap.

She tucked her face against his neck, sucking in great gulps of air. She shivered beneath the light shawl she wore and Cal could do nothing for her except wrap his arms tighter around her shoulders.

"Talk to me, Megan." He kept his voice steady. "Why did you leave the tour? What's going on?"

She shivered again and then grew quiet. She wrapped her arms around his waist and turned her head so her soft, warm breath brushed his chin.

"She was there; on the tour."

"Who?"

"Laurie McCluer," she said on a sigh, her voice sounding resigned to some fate Cal couldn't comprehend.

"Who? Someone hassled you on the tour? Is that why you…" his voice trailed off as it dawned on him who she was talking about.

"Are you fucking kidding me?" He pushed her away from him so he could look at her face.

Her skin was pale in the meager light and bits of hair had come loose from her netting. Her cheek was icy and clammy as he brushed the curl back. But it was her eyes, glittering in what little light there was, that told him she was frightened. Wide open, pupils dilated, she stared at him as though seeing someone else. Her gaze darted to the left and right, searching. She blinked. When she looked back at him, her gaze had cleared and he could tell she actually saw him, instead of some ghost from the past.

She laughed shakily. "Never mind. It's just my silly imagination. You know, living in the house and hearing the story."

Cal didn't want to ridicule her, even though he knew there were no ghosts. He thought to tease her instead. "Are you afraid of the dark, Megan Sue? Is that why you don't like doing this tour?"

She stood, tugging her shawl around her like armor. "I am not, but I don't like any tour on god-awful damp and foggy nights like this." She shivered.

"Then let's get you somewhere warm." He tucked her close to his side and started walking back toward the pub.

"Oh, God! I can't go there. I left them all before the end of the tour." Megan tried to stop but he continued to tug her along. "Jeff is going to kill me."

"Naw, he'll just fire you," Cal quipped but upon seeing her distress, he recanted. "He won't, believe me. Besides, I told the other guy to finish the story over a beer."

He didn't go into the Pub, but steered Megan around the corner to his truck. She started to protest but he simply opened the door, lifted her onto the seat and tucked all her petticoats and long dress in with her. Instead of closing the door, he leaned in for a kiss, warming her chilly lips with his until she began kissing him back in earnest.

"Let's go over to my place," he whispered as he feathered kisses across her cheek. "I think it's time I found out just how many petticoats you actually do wear under that skirt of yours."

Chapter 8

It was easy enough for Megan to forget what she had heard in the park – what she *thought* she heard – when Cal got her into his condo. This time she knew there would be no interruptions as she watched him deliberately shut off his phone and put it in the drawer with his gun.

When he walked toward her, she felt as if she were being stalked. His eyes glittered silver in the dim light. Although she was within an inch or two of his height, when he reached for her, she felt small and delicate. She quit thinking at all when his mouth descended on hers. All she could do was feel…

Heat, from his hands as they slid up and down her bare arms. Arousal, as his tongue flicked out and traced the seam of her lips. Passion surfaced and fascination ran alongside as he took her mouth in a provocative kiss. It was unlike anything she had experienced before, and she was very curious to see where it would lead.

Always being an active participant when it came to physical contact sports, she slid her hands around his back, tugging his shirt out of his jeans. His skin was warm to the touch and she could feel him quiver as she explored taut muscles. Suddenly anxious to feel more of him against her, she moved to the front, quickly unbuttoning his shirt and sliding it off his shoulders. When she reached for the button on his pants, he stopped her hands with his.

"Slow down," he whispered as his hot tongue traced the shell of her ear. "We have all the time in the world."

"I want you."

Three simple words that had Cal groaning, but he refused to rush. "The word of the night is *savor*." He kissed along her neck, nipped her collar bone, then moved back to her chin, up to her mouth.

Her mouth was a gift from the gods. Full lips, wide and sensuous; he felt he could spend his life just kissing her. Even though the rest of his body was, like her, aching for more. This time when his tongue queried, she opened to him. He plundered, yet she gave in return and the world spun out of control. Lust swirled low in his belly and he was hard and stiff and aching to rip off his jeans and take her right there on the living room floor.

There might be a time for fast and furious, but not tonight. While he knew there were no such things as ghosts, he wouldn't discount her worries. He would simply chase them away and make her think only of him.

He took her hand and led her to the bedroom where he began slowly undressing her. As her skirt, then each petticoat fell to the floor, the night, the fog, the worries fell away, too.

"Why did women think they needed so many clothes?" Cal whispered as he lifted her top and feathered kisses across her midriff.

"Perhaps to make the quest all the harder for the men," she answered. He felt a shiver go through her as his fingers slid down the back of her legs, pulling her closer as his teeth nipped her stomach.

"No amount of fabric could keep me from this prize." He hooked his thumbs into her panties and slid them down. He kept exploring her soft skin, tickling her belly button with his tongue, tantalizing her with kisses but never going further down. Not that he didn't want to, but he knew if he did, he would lose control and end things too quickly.

"Oh, lordy," Megan gasped, her legs shaking. "I can't stand if you do that."

"No need," he murmured. As he stood, he snagged her top and slid it up and off. She wore a lacy camisole which was gone as quickly. He pushed her gently onto the bed.

"You are so beautiful," he breathed the words softly as his gaze flicked from her high breasts, down to a narrow waist and flat stomach, lower still to a thatch of dark hair and incredibly long legs. He was almost afraid to touch her, afraid she would disappear and he would have only his dreams.

His words caused a flush to spread slowly until her entire body glowed.

"Has no one ever told you that?" he asked as he kicked off his shoes and removed his pants.

"You used to say my legs were too long and I was as clumsy as a new colt." She tried to pout but he could see the corners of her mouth tilt.

"And look how wrong I was." He lay down beside her and took her in his arms, molding her to him. In that instant he felt totally at peace. It wasn't the thought of making love to Megan. Instead, he realized that she was what had been missing from his life. She was sunshine in the face of the darkness in which he sometimes worked. She was the calm to his temper.

He proceeded to show her just exactly how perfect they were together. He let his lips travel her body, and the more he explored, the more she groaned, and whimpered and squirmed.

"Please," she begged.

"Slowly savor," he replied as he sucked on her nipple, tonguing the tip until it was hard.

Her back arched, her fingers clawed his shoulders but he wouldn't relent. He wanted, *needed* to appease his hunger for her, and that meant traveling every inch of her body with his hands; his mouth.

Her skin was satin to the touch, bronze from the sun, and with a scent he couldn't identify but that was uniquely Megan. He continued his quest downward until she tugged on his hair.

"Cal." His name was a plea and he relented, rolling over until he was cradled between her thighs.

"What do you want, darling?" He leaned on his elbows and gazed at her, his breath stopping.

Her eyes were glazed with passion and he could feel her chest heave as she gasped for breath. Her hands were everywhere, sliding down his back then grabbing his ass.

"You are so totally not playing fair," she said. She slid one hand between their hips. "You never were very good about sharing the fun," she added just as she latched onto him and squeezed.

His head dropped to her forehead as he sucked in a breath. "What I did wasn't fun for you?" he managed to gasp.

Her hand slowly slid down his length, then back up. "Not when I can't touch you in return." She turned her head and bit his earlobe. His control flew out the window.

With a growl, he rocked back on his haunches and pushed her legs apart.

Megan almost giggled. He looked so fierce, looming above her. She had wanted to make him forget the savoring and take her fast. But now, as his hands slid down her thighs and his thumbs came together at her apex, she wondered.

"Wait," she gasped. "I wasn't done with you."

"Next time," he growled, tucking his arms beneath her knees and lifting; plunging into her until he could go no further. He stopped, groaning, then bent forward and kissed her, his tongue tracing her lips before sliding inside.

Megan felt every inch of him and wondered how they had even fit. At first he didn't move and time hung suspended.

"God, you feel incredible." He pulled out just a little and plunged back in. "So tight." He repeated the movement, rubbing just right against her and the tingles began. She found herself lifting her hips to match his rhythm and he sank deeper. Each time he pulled out, the slide back in had her trembling.

When the rhythm changed, she knew he was close, and she deliberately clutched her muscles around him. As he changed the angle of his penetration just slightly, Megan knew she would go over the edge with him.

"Now, baby, now," he whispered urgently.

Her body lifted to his, her heels pushed into his back as he carried her over and they plunged off the summit. The climax took over her entire body, blood racing hot through her veins, muscles shaking as wave after wave of ecstasy washed over her. Even after he collapsed against her the aftershocks kept her on the edge. If anyone had ever told her something like this was possible, she would have laughed. Now, she knew she would never again settle for less. She hugged him tight then lightly scratched his back.

"Ah, that feels good," he mumbled against her neck as her muscles continued contracting around him. "And I don't mean the back scratch."

Long moments later, Cal reached over and flipped off the bedside lamp, cocooning them in darkness and Megan fell asleep in his arms, no dreams disrupting her slumber.

* * *

"Hello, sleepyhead." Cal looked up from the bacon he was frying as Megan came into the kitchen. She was dressed in only her panties and his tee-shirt, and given her height, that barely skimmed her hips. All completely fine with him, he thought, as he tugged her close for a kiss. She was still warm from bed and he thought to take her right back there.

"Mmm," she murmured against his mouth. "Thanks for letting me sleep in."

Cal snorted. "Six-thirty is letting you sleep in?" He flipped the bacon out on a paper towel then cracked several eggs into the grease.

"What?" Megan squawked, swiveling around to find the clock on the stove. Then she punched him in the arm. "It's the middle of the night!"

"Hey, some of us have to work for a living," he said as he plated the eggs, then added toast and bacon. "Grab some silverware."

She followed him into the dining room and sat with a huff. He put down the plates then went back to retrieve coffee, putting a big mug in front of her.

"Thanks," she said gratefully as she took a swallow. She didn't say another word until she had eaten everything he had put on her plate and even snatched one of his pieces of toast.

He raised a brow.

"Sorry. Sex makes me hungry."

"Too bad I can't go for round two," he said.

She gave him a grin. "That would cost you lunch."

"I can afford the lunch. I just can't afford the time right now."

A look came over Megan's face. "Geez, I totally forgot about your case. What happened out at Porchello? Have they found the murderer?"

"Ha. I wish it had been that easy, then I wouldn't have to deal with Barney and the little rascals."

"Did you watch a lot of television when you were young? You seem to have an affinity for referring to old sitcoms."

Cal drained his coffee cup. "Barney found some witnesses named Tom, Dick and Harry."

"So did every Tom, Dick and Harry know who did John Dough in?" She started laughing.

Cal had to admit the irony of it all. "You don't know the half of it. The sheriff called them witnesses but they didn't know squat. It's all a computer game; winner takes all and they take instructions from some guy they don't know named Simon."

Megan's face went blank for a minute, then she totally cracked up, tears running down her cheeks from her laughter. "Simon Says?" It set her off again.

"Ha, ha. I'm glad you find my craziness humorous."

"It's just...so..." She stopped with her mouth open. "Wait a minute. Did you say they were playing a computer game?"

"Yeah, but a computer wasn't responsible for bashing in Dough's head." Cal got up and brought back the coffee pot, refilling both their cups.

"Tell me about the game." Megan grabbed his arm as he sat.

"I knew you should have been there," he said, "but no, you had to do your civic duty by Jeff."

Megan shook her head. "Don't even think about getting into a spitting contest with your brother."

Cal wiggled his brows. "Would I win?"

"Not going there," Megan said. "Tell me about the game."

Cal had to think for a moment, trying to remember what the boys had said. "It's something about *Monopoly* and *Survivor*," he told Megan. "They cheat on each other and do a lot of double-crossing from what I gathered."

"A computer simulation; not just a game." Megan nodded her head, apparently understanding more than Cal did and she hadn't even been there.

"What's the difference?"

"A game is like, say, *Solitaire*. There's a specific beginning and a definite end. You play against the computer and you win or you lose. A simulation, however, has no real end and there are a lot of players, all playing against each other. You get to a point and make a decision that leads you to another point. Depending on the decision you made, you progress or fall back, but you get to keep going, until you lose whatever assets the game is played for." She paused, "Or sometimes until you die...metaphorically speaking," she quickly added.

"Just because John Dough might have been playing the game doesn't mean he was killed because of it," Cal stated.

"Perhaps not, but can you say for sure?"

"These boys have jumped to the conclusion that Dough was in the game because he's dead and someone is missing *from* the game. We don't know if the two are connected."

Megan twirled a strand of hair and Cal momentarily forgot the case and remembered how soft her hair felt against his chest. He reached over and slid his fingers through the thickness, using it to tug her closer.

"Maybe I should just call in sick to work," he said, bending in for a kiss.

Megan put a finger to his lips to stop him. "Was there anything else about the simulation? What do they play for? Where does the game take place – a real place or an imaginary world?"

82

Cal raised a brow. He was losing his touch if she wanted to talk computers.

"Cal?"

He shrugged as he stood and gathered their dishes. "Something about a mine." He said as he walked to the kitchen.

"Minecraft?" Megan said and he could hear the excitement in her voice.

"Yeah, that was it. Why?"

"That is awesome. It adds a whole new dimension to the game." She came over and grabbed his arm. "You have to get me into that computer simulation."

"I can't have a civilian working on a police case." He frowned.

"At least let me get a look at his computer," she pumped, as though he hadn't already said no.

"Megan."

"You do have it, don't you?"

Chapter 9

So much for his own game, Cal thought later that afternoon. He had dropped Megan off at the B&B and driven to the federal office building. He had checked with the department but the kid's computer hadn't been with his effects. That meant he'd have to get it from the family.

He found Commissioner Dough in his office, which he thought strange given his son had died just days ago. He learned he was a widower, and figured people grieved in different ways, but after talking to the man, he wondered. It hadn't taken long to realize that the man either didn't know much about his son's activities, or he wasn't saying for fear of smearing his own name. He did get permission to get the computer from the house and headed that way.

He thought about calling Barney, but the minute he thought it, he told himself that was not going to happen. If the man had information, let him call Cal. The same with the boys he had interviewed. But hours later with three BPD tech guys comparing notes, they had only been able to get into Dough's email, not into any game.

* * *

Megan came upstairs early that evening dressed in jeans and a tee shirt, her hair pulled back in a tail. There was no tour scheduled and she hoped to have time with Stacy, who was carefully lifting a sheet of cookies from the oven.

"Those smell yummy." Megan snatched one as soon as Stacy had shuffled them to the rack.

"Going out?" her friend asked just as Megan's phone beeped.

She read the text. "Apparently not. Cal's on the way over."

Stacy frowned. "It's too late for dinner."

Megan laughed. "I'm sure he doesn't come over just for dinner."

"You haven't been here the last few years." She grinned when she said it. "I love my brothers dearly but there are some days—"

"When you just can't get enough of us," Cal finished her sentence as he came in the door.

"Hmm, right." Stacy turned to put more dough on the sheet and Cal snitched three hot ones off the rack.

"And stay out of my cookies," she said, not even turning around.

"You sound just like mom." He glanced at his sister, then quickly gave Megan a kiss.

"I saw that," Stacy said as she turned.

"Damn, you *are* Mom."

"Speaking of, she called and wanted to know when you were going out to see them. Dad needs a golf partner."

"I'm in the middle of a case," he replied, then frowned. "Why didn't she call me?"

Stacy pinned him with a glare. "Maybe because you never answer your phone?"

Megan just shook her head. It had always been that way with the Garrett family. Their loving, sibling banter had been some consolation to her when she had moved in with them all those years ago.

"Is that it?" she asked, pointing to the laptop Cal had tucked under his arm. He had said in his text he needed her help.

He handed it over and went to the fridge for a couple of beers. Megan sat down at the breakfast nook, opened the computer and booted it up. Cal opened a beer and handed it to her, then opened his own. When the desktop appeared, Megan sat the beer aside and perused his icons.

"The guys downtown couldn't come up with much."

"I can see why," Megan answered, looking closely. "He has so many programs and games it's hard to say which the right one is."

Stacy came over to the table. "What's going on?"

"There's a computer game that we're trying to get into," Megan began but Cal quickly interrupted.

"That's all; just a game," he said.

"You should have Matt look at it. He's a wiz with computers," his sister said.

"Police business."

She frowned. "Well, Megan's looking at it." She turned back to the counter.

"That's my business. Don't you have cookies to bake?"

Megan looked up. "That's mean," she whispered.

"That's right," Stacy said, apparently overhearing. "One of these days, I may not be here for you to be mean to."

"I'll find you, wherever you go," Cal said in a deep dangerous voice. "I'm the detective you know."

Megan kicked him under the table. When he looked at her in surprise, she jerked her head toward Stacy. She stood at the sink, head down. With a sigh, Cal got up and went to his sister, enveloping her petite frame in a massive hug.

"Hey, pigtails," he said, kissing the top of her head. "I would find you, you know. I'd go through heaven and hell. Not because I'm a detective, but because I'm your brother."

Megan felt tears in the corner of her eyes. When Stacy turned, she saw tears there, too.

"You'll never get into heaven," Stacy teased.

Cal kissed her forehead this time. "I would, but only because I love you."

Megan didn't bother excusing herself but rushed out of the room for the bathroom. She leaned weakly against the door, tears streaming down her face, lips trembling. When she splashed cool water on her face and looked in the mirror, she saw the truth. She was in love with Cal Garrett. Not the infatuation of her teens. This was grown-up, heart-can-be-broken, gut wrenching love.

He was so much more than just a handsome guy. He cared about and protected the people and city where he lived, and that went well beyond the call of duty. While he might have a temper and little patience, she had seen him with the boys on the boat. His temper came from fear that harm would come. And now…few men of her acquaintance would so openly express their feelings, even if it was to family.

When she pulled herself together and went back to the kitchen, Cal was at the table and Stacy was at the counter, making him a sandwich and chattering away.

Back to normal, she thought. Hoping to keep her own feelings hidden because they were much too fragile and new, she ducked her head and concentrated on the computer. She tried every hack she could think of, but she couldn't locate the game.

Somewhere down the hall, she heard the clock. When it struck twelve, she surfaced with a jerk. It couldn't be midnight already. Quickly glancing around, Stacy was nowhere in sight but Cal still sat across from her.

However, when she looked, his head was tipped back against the wall and his eyes were closed. She smiled when a gentle snore floated her way.

"So much for a hot date," she said softly.

"Huh? What?" Cal jerked awake. He rubbed both hands over his face.

"I can't find anything. Do you think we can talk to the boys tomorrow?"

Cal rolled his shoulders and turned his head from side to side. She heard a crack as his neck popped. She had to think how uncomfortable he must have been for the hours she was on the computer.

"You need to go home and get some sleep."

His brows rose. "I could just sleep here with you."

She smiled but shook her head. "I'm not ready to play that card with your sister."

* * *

Cal picked Megan up at eight, handing her a large latte when she climbed in the truck.

"Ah, I am happily your slave," she cooed after the first swallow.

He slammed the gears back into park. "We're not going to Porchello." He reached over and cupped her neck, pulling her to him. The kiss, drugging as it was, did nothing to dampen his libido so he lifted a hand to her breast. She was warm and firm and he could feel the nipple pebble beneath her bra.

She pushed at him. "It's an expression," she laughed as she straightened.

"I'm a literal kind of guy." He reached for her again, but she just grinned as she swatted his hand away and took another drink of coffee.

With a sigh, he pulled out of the parking lot and into traffic. Sparrow Drive was the shits during commute, but he was really in no hurry. He was on the clock, but getting to spend his time with Megan was a bonus. He glanced at her and she turned toward him and smiled. He had sudden misgivings about taking her with him to Porchello. She was a beautiful young woman and he would have to keep a sharp eye on Tom, Dick and Harry.

He pulled into the pancake house and got out, coming around to open Megan's door.

"A latte and breakfast, too?" She grinned as she hopped down. "What a guy."

"Coffee makes you a smart ass," he returned, taking her elbow and steering her toward the door. "I told the boys to meet us here and get a corner booth in the back so we can have a conversation and not be disturbed."

When he opened the door, it took a minute to find the kids. As he threaded his way between tables, he saw them all scoot around the booth and jump up. A little respect, he thought, but then noticed that all eyes were on Megan.

"Sit your butts down," he growled.

Harold blushed clear to his red hair. "After the lady." He put out a hand. "Ma'am?"

Megan squeezed Cal's hand, surprisingly hard. "Be nice," she whispered as she slid into the booth. The boys crowded in on one side and Cal sat on the outside next to Megan.

"Hello," Megan said, extending her hand. "I'm Megan Anderson." That should have been enough, Cal thought, but no, she had to smile. God, he had forgotten what it was like to be twenty. All three boys stammered out their names, reaching out for the opportunity to touch a goddess. No, he hadn't forgotten. But this goddess belonged to him and he let them know it, shooting each a murderous look.

Megan patted his leg under the table. How does she do it, he wondered? Just a soft look or a touch, and he was putty in her hands.

"Detective Garrett said you were helping on the case," Richard said.

She smiled, again, and Cal gritted his teeth as the boys all but drooled. If any of them were guilty as far as Dough was concerned, they would surely slip up around Megan. He needed to concentrate.

"Detective Garrett is handling the case," Megan replied to Richard's comment. "I want in the game."

The boys looked surprised. "I don't know," Harry said. "It's been going on awhile and you need an invitation."

She handed him a card. "Get me one."

He looked at the card and grinned. "Mystic87? You should use Mystic Goddess."

"Hey, watch it." Cal leaned forward, getting right in his face.

Another pat on the leg, this time with a little squeeze.

"Tell me about the game," Megan said, and suddenly everyone was all business. Cal listened, but didn't quite get all the details as they spoke of avatars and blogs.

"Is it UGC?" she asked.

"What's that?" Cal asked.

"User generated content," Tom answered. "But in reply to Miss Anderson's question, it would only be considered UGC within the game because we can construct barriers that prevent others from penetrating our fortress. It's not privy to anyone outside the game."

"Hmm." Megan looked thoughtful. "Tell me more."

"You have to have a hypothetical treasure that is somehow connected to the place you live. You build a fortress, adding more barriers for each time someone asks a wrong question. A piece of barrier goes down if someone gets a question right."

"Are all the treasures hypothetical?" Megan asked.

"Hypothetical is probably the wrong word," Dick said. "The treasure should be some obscure artifact." Seeing her expression, he went on. "Just the other day, we took a player out of the game by discovering he lived in Santa Fe and his artifact was a long buried trove of Navajo Indian pottery."

"Wow." Megan leaned back. "So now you own the pottery as well as the artifacts you brought to the game."

Cal was hypnotized. Not only was Megan beautiful, but so smart it made his head hurt. Her eyes glowed with excitement as she talked to the boys. Artifacts meant history, but he wasn't about to tell her that. She had no use for history, but apparently buried treasure was a different matter – if it was buried in a computer game.

"What was Dough's artifact?" she asked.

"We don't know. We think he went by the name Doughboy," Tom said, "which isn't very original, but other than that, we hadn't found out much about him other than he lived on the coast."

"How do you know that?" Cal asked.

"The fortress you construct has to be near the obscure treasure, but in the building, you have to incorporate things that give hints as to the location. In this case, he had a dock with a boat tied to it."

Cal frowned. "That could be anywhere near water."

"Exactly," said Harold. "But his fortress is surrounded by water."

"Which would mean he lives on, or near, an island." Cal was beginning to think he could get into this. "Can you help us find his artifact if we accessed his computer? It might help determine why he was killed."

They shrugged. "We could try," said Dick, "but everybody's computer is password protected.

"We're past that," Cal said as he slid out of the booth. "I'll be right back."

Megan watched him leave, glad for a few minute's reprieve. She had the feeling Cal would swallow the boys whole if she didn't keep a hand on his leg. She didn't think it only had to do with the case, but couldn't pinpoint what was making him so edgy. She turned to the boys with a smile.

"Have you eaten? No? Well, let's order breakfast, on Detective Garrett."

Their food arrived just as Cal returned. He slid the laptop on the seat to the other side of her and didn't say a word as he dove into the chef's special she had ordered for him. Maybe that would appease the beast within, she thought with a smile.

"Thanks for the breakfast, Detective," Harold said politely and the other two murmured their thanks, too.

"What?" He turned his gaze on her. He raised a brow, but his eyes twinkled.

"I didn't bring my purse," she said just to him. "I'll repay you if you want."

He made a show of reaching across her for the laptop, his head turned to whisper in her ear. "Oh, you're going to pay, all right."

Her lower regions tingled in awareness. It was a really tough toss-up for her – sex with Cal or delving into the world of cybercrime. Well, there really wasn't a choice, she thought, seeing as she was sitting with three impressionable young men who thought she and Cal were going to solve a crime. She concentrated on booting up the computer as the waitress cleared away the plates.

"We got in, but I can't determine which of his programs is the game," Megan said as she turned the computer to the right and scooted around the booth toward the boys. They crowded together to look at the screen. Richard took over the keyboard.

He's good, Megan thought, as his fingers flew. Screens popped up and then were gone as he browsed.

"Try here," Tom pointed to something on the screen, then pushed a function key. The screen went black.

"What the fuck?" Richard said.

"Hey," Cal cautioned, and Megan smiled. It wasn't as though she had never heard that word before. Besides which, he had scooted around as close to Megan as he could, but she didn't think he could see the computer screen from that angle.

"Sorry," Richard apologized, "but there's nothing there."

"What do you mean, there's nothing? The screen is full of icons." Cal waved a hand toward the computer.

"The game disappeared," explained Harold. "It was right there, and when we tried to open it, it was gone."

Tom had pulled up his own laptop and was madly tapping on keys. In just minutes, he gave a sign of relief. "The game's still there. I can access my fortress."

"So someone has just deleted it from Dough's computer?" Cal questioned. "Who knows he's gone, besides you three?" He was instantly all detective and Megan could hear the authority in his voice.

The boys shook their heads. "There's been nothing on the message board or chat rooms."

Cal signaled for the ticket and gave the waitress some bills. He slid out of the booth and Megan followed as the boys slid out the other side.

"What should we do?" asked Harold.

"Outside," was all Cal would say as he turned and led the way. Once they were in the parking lot, he turned to the boys.

"Don't say a word about any of this on any list, blog, message board, or whatever you're on." He looked from boy to boy. "Don't talk about it among yourselves online, either. You have something to say, you call me."

It was hard hearing the frustration in Cal's voice, knowing he was trying to solve a crime with as many variables as players in the game. Megan had to find a way to help.

"Get me in that game," she said to the boys as they parted ways.

Chapter 10

Megan spent the afternoon helping Stacy get ready for the evening tour. She would have rather spent it with Cal, but he was chasing down a lead on another case.

Since they didn't know if she would get an invitation to the game, or how long it would take, she kept her laptop on the kitchen table as they worked. Besides, the internet signal was non-existent in the basement.

The email address on her card was one which she had only used when investigative reporting and she had told the boys they could contact her through it. Since they knew her 'handle' and she knew theirs, they had agreed to a "hands-off" to each other's treasure, and instead would concentrate on the other players in the game.

Ping. Megan put down the glass she was drying and looked at her computer screen. Email from an unknown source.

She opened the file and read. "Yes!"

The email gave her the information needed to enter the game. The temporary password would expire in an hour, so she had to get in, set up her account and change her password before she could play.

"I don't understand why some online game is so important," Stacy commented as Megan abandoned the dish drying for the computer.

"You sound like your brother," Megan said as she continued typing.

"I mean, it's not like I don't use the computer. I shop on line all the time, and do Facebook and email."

Megan smiled. Her friend was a totally social person. It was unfortunate that there was another side to the internet that wasn't so bright and sunny.

"Gaming can be fun but in this case, someone is trying to hurt people and if I can use my skills to help Cal find that, I will."

Stacy looked at her in surprise. "You're not supposed to tell me. Cal will be mad."

Megan grimaced. It was just so natural to tell Stacy things. They had been friends for life. "Promise not to say anything?"

Stacy nodded. "I don't know enough about it to say anything. I know just enough to post to Facebook. I have Matt doing the B&B website."

Megan looked up. "Is that how you met him?"

Stacy nodded. "He was recommended by a guest. Mom and Dad hadn't seen the necessity of having a website, but in this day and age, it's important. I do know that much."

Ping.

"I'm in," Megan said under her breath. Now the work began. She had already decided her obscure artifact would be a large cache of British gold supposedly buried near the Parker River. Now, she had to start building her fortress without giving away the location.

Lost in the game, hours went by. She recognized Harold's avatar, seeking entrance, but she knew he was just doing it to pull her into the game.

"Megan?"

"Megan?" Stacy said again.

It took her a minute to focus. Outside, the sun was setting, long shadows stretching across the back yard. The kitchen lights were on. An empty glass of water sat at her right, but she didn't remember drinking it.

"What time is it?" She stretched, pulling her hands over her head and bending back and forth.

"After seven. You need to get ready for the tour."

Megan blinked, looking at her friend. Stacy was dressed in her historic costume, complete with little dust mop.

"Oh, god, I completely forgot." Her mind was still building and seeking out information on other fortresses. It would take a bit to reboot to the present, much less to put herself back into 1776 mode. "I need a shower." She carefully shut down the laptop. She texted Cal and told him about her progress, then headed downstairs.

It was funny, she thought as she dressed. Jeff had asked her if she wanted to do the river tour or one downtown that evening and she had actually said the river. She worried that the ghost would make an appearance, and at the same time, almost hoped she would. It was crazy, hoping she would see a ghost, but something about the whole story drew her in. Almost like her investigative reporting or the online game – the more one knew, the more there was to find out.

She came upstairs to find the kitchen full of people, all in re-enactor dress except for one.

"Excuse me, but that's mine." She pushed the lid down on the laptop she had left on the table and glared at Matt.

He gave her a smile, not in the least bothered by her icy tone.

"I was just admiring it. All the latest bells and whistles, huh?" He stood, moving very, very close to Megan. "I hear you're a computer aficionado. Maybe we should get together and compare notes." Another smile, this time obviously suggestive.

Megan hadn't really thought about Stacy's boyfriend one way or the other, but now she wondered how she would tell her best friend that he had come on to her. Maybe she would have Cal run a check on him, if he hadn't already.

"Are we ready?" Toni bounced over to ask. She was as bubbly tonight as on all the other nights Megan had seen her. She wondered sometimes if she took pep pills. As a group, they moved into the sitting room to greet their guests.

Tonight's group was as lively as Toni and Megan was quickly pulled into their chatter. Everyone was a member of the Briggs family reunion. The parents lived in Boston and kids, grandkids and even some great-grandkids had all come back for their seventieth wedding anniversary party.

The elder Briggs had stayed home, but the rest were lighthearted as they trotted down the steps of the B&B and into the night.

As Megan led them along the designated path, the moon full and bright, she wondered what it would be like to have such a large happy family. Being an only child, she hadn't felt the lack of family while her parents were alive, but now? For just an instant before she started her monologue, she thought of what it would be like having a family with Cal; of actually being part of the Garrett family instead of always standing just a little to the outside. But that was another fairy tale, just like the one she was about to tell.

* * *

What did it say about her, Megan wondered later, when she found herself disappointed that Laurie's ghost hadn't appeared on the tour? She felt like she had when researching an undercover story and on the edge of discovery. Something was out there; something she couldn't put her finger on, but every instinct she had was on alert as she led the group the last block to the pub.

Maybe Cal was right and there was no ghost; that it was all a figment of her imagination. She saw Cal sitting at the bar, waiting for her, and thought maybe she just needed a distraction. She headed in his direction, but the conversations around her reminded her she was still on the clock.

Males, young and old alike, heartily joked about being among the patriots, while the women sighed over the heroic Logan Mallory and the tragic end of his love. There were always more questions, to which she demurely kept repeating the words *legend* and *folk lore*.

"I'd be a patriot," said one young boy between slurps of his soft drink. "Those British soldiers wouldn't tell me what to do."

His father smiled indulgently. "I tell you what to do."

"You're my dad. That's different."

"Not as much as you might think." Megan stood to the side of their table. "The British government was like your parents in some ways. It had provided the people who immigrated here with the means to get here, to start businesses, and offered them an outlet for the products they produced." She smiled at the boy, who was gazing at her with wide eyes. "Sort of like your parents giving you a home, food, taking you places."

She bent down low and whispered. "Would you repay them by rebelling?"

He slowly shook his head, then looked up at her. "But I can move out or go to college and be on my own. Then they can't tell me what to do anymore."

She chuckled. "That's right. And the colonists wanted to be on their own, but they couldn't agree with the British king as to the rules."

He seemed to think about that, then his face brightened. "They should have compromised, like we do when I want something and my parents think it's bad for me."

His dad ruffled his hair. "You would make a great Parliamentarian, son."

Megan moved on. She realized that whether the story was based on fact, or was totally fiction, it did lead to discussions of democracy, diplomacy and personal rights. She had to wonder why people today kept repeating history's mistakes instead of learning from them.

"Is there really treasure here?" asked a man at another table.

Megan tilted her head slightly. The man had an accent, but she couldn't place it. He sat off to one side in the shadows, but he would have been able to hear the conversations around him. He hadn't been on the tour, she thought, although the script never actually said anything about a treasure. Still, there was no reason to evade his question.

"There is a lot of research on lost and hidden treasure, not just in the Boston area, but all over the world. For more than that, I guess you'd have to go to the library." She smiled politely and turned to leave but the man caught her forearm, holding her in place.

* * *

Cal had been watching as Megan played the ultimate host – smiling, laughing, taking time to talk to everyone and listening as one of the young kids proclaimed his allegiance to the patriot cause. He smiled, recalling having said similar words in his youth.

Now he tensed when a man at a far table grabbed her arm. He had just taken a step in her direction when the beer on the man's table tipped over, the cold brew spilling into his lap.

Megan gasped, the man swore, and Cal sat back down. *Karma*, he thought as the bartender hurried over with a towel.

Megan turned and he caught her eye, but she was frowning. Her lips were moving but no words emerged as she paused in front of him. He spread his legs and she stepped between them. He loosely looped his arms around her waist and leaned forward to give her a kiss. When he leaned back, she was still frowning.

"Hi, Cal, I'm so happy to see you," he mocked.

"Hmm?" For the first time she actually looked at him.

"What's up?" he asked.

"That guy." She nodded slightly over her shoulder.

"Yeah. If he hadn't spilled his beer, I would have been in his face."

"He didn't," she said.

"Didn't what?"

"Spill his beer. When he grabbed my arm, the beer just…just spilled." Her forehead creased.

Cal looked back to the corner but the man was gone.

"Why did he grab you in the first place?" The thought that anyone would put their hands on Megan made him see red.

"He was asking about treasure. Even though we never say anything about treasure, everyone always wants to know about treasure." She laughed lightly, as though trying to lighten her own mood. "Speaking of, I'm in the game and have hidden my treasure very well, if I do say so myself."

Cal had questions about whether the game would get them anywhere, but at the moment it was the only lead to Dough's murder. He also had serious misgivings about Megan being in the game, but as long as he was close by, he knew nobody would get to her. Besides, it was on a computer, not real life. However, work wasn't exactly what he had on his mind at the moment.

"Are you done here?"

She looked around. "Actually, yes. We always leave one person with the group, in case anyone needs help finding their way back to their vehicles, but—"

He stopped her with a kiss. "I have a sudden urge to rip your clothes off," he whispered then nipped her ear lobe.

"Well," she said, her smile once again bright. "I certainly don't think that would be a good idea here."

He stood, grabbing her hand and leading her to the door. "That's what I thought."

* * *

The minute the door to the condo closed behind them, he had her up against the wall. His hands were everywhere and Megan could do no more than melt into his embrace. Hot lips wandered from her mouth down the vee of her bodice. His tongue lapped along her chemise and his hands gathered up her skirts to touch her bare legs. "What is it about your costume that turns me on?" His words brought Megan out of the sensual haze.

"It wasn't an accident," she murmured.

"Hmm?" Cal's head was down, his fingers now working on the buttons of her bodice.

She palmed his cheeks, lifting his head so he looked at her.

"The beer; it wasn't an accident," she said in a rush. "It was Laurie."

"What are you talking about?"

She brushed his hands aside when he tried to remove her bodice.

"She's shown up at the river on every tour I've done, until tonight," Megan said as she paced away from Cal. She couldn't think when he had his hands on her. "She's trying to tell me something but I haven't figured it out yet. She wasn't at the river, but was at the Pub and she spills that man's beer." She spun around to face Cal. "Why would she do that? Was she trying to warn me about him?"

Cal's gaze narrowed. "I'm trying to make love to you and you're talking about a fucking ghost that doesn't even exist?"

Megan took a step back at the anger in his voice. She might have felt the same way in the beginning but there were too many coincidences.

"I think she does."

Cal ran his hands through his hair. "It's just a stupid figment of your imagination."

Megan couldn't believe he had just said that. Her hands shook as she buttoned her blouse. "I'm going home."

"No, wait." Cal reached her in a heartbeat but she shook off his grip. "I didn't mean it that way, Megan."

"It doesn't matter. You said it."

She reached the door but he slammed a hand against it when she tried to open it.

"I want to go, Cal." Her voice was deadly quiet.

"I'll drive you."

"I can get there myself."

"I said I would drive," he growled, grabbing his keys.

It was the longest ten minutes of Megan's life. Cal said nothing; simply scowled out the window. She kept her face averted, too hurt to say anything she might regret.

The minute he put the truck in park, she opened the door. She didn't look at him when he grabbed her arm.

"I didn't mean that the way it sounded, Megan. But you know there just are no such things."

She did turn then. "I would have said the same thing weeks ago. Now I think different." She tried very hard not

101

to cry. "If you can't believe in me, there's not much left to say."

She jumped down and ran to the house.

"Megan!" He called her name, but she didn't turn back. She couldn't; not with tears streaming down her cheeks.

* * *

Megan tossed and turned most of the night before falling into an exhausted sleep, which meant she overslept. As she showered she worried what Stacy would say because she couldn't remember if she had promised to help with breakfast.

As she brushed the tangles out of her hair, she thought about Cal. She loved him; she knew that with all her heart. She loved that he took his job seriously, even as she worried every day that he could get hurt. She respected what he did and she would never ask him to give that up. But there was just no hope for a relationship if he couldn't do the same and accept her…everything about her.

Which made her ask herself the question, why was she so adamant about the ghost? Had she really seen all those things, and why, if there *was* a ghost, had it decided to share with her? If only someone else saw what she saw.

If, if, if, she thought as she wandered upstairs. If only Laurie had decided to plague someone else entirely.

Her phone pinged. She looked at it then tucked it into her pocket. He was up to ten texts and three calls. She had counted, yes, but refused to read them, much less answer them.

"I have never in my life known my brother to send flowers," Stacy said the minute Megan walked into the kitchen. "Not even to Mom."

"What?" Megan's gaze followed the direction Stacy pointed. On the kitchen table, under the window, was a beautiful vase of daisies. Not roses, she thought, the ultimate apology flower, but bright yellow and white daisies. She tried not to smile, but couldn't help it. Daisies were her very favorite flower.

"How do you know they're from Cal?"

"I looked at the card," Stacy said with a shrug. "He could have written something besides his name."

"Did you tell him those were my favorite?" she asked Stacy as she poured a cup of coffee.

"Are you kidding? If my brother's in relationship trouble -- and chances are he's in deep shit if he sent flowers -- I would not help him out." She handed Megan a piece of coffee cake. "Let him wallow."

"I'm sorry if I was supposed to help this morning," Megan said as they sat, but Stacy waved away her apology.

"Jeff was over so I made him serve." She grinned. "It's his fault anyway, that we're booked to capacity every day. Not that I'm complaining." She had her elbows on the table, holding her mug with two hands. "Who would ever have thought such a simple tour would bring in such great business."

"I'm really happy for you guys," Megan said, then frowned. "You're not going to kick me out and rent my room, are you?"

Stacy laughed. "Downstairs is definitely off limits. I need a place to hide at times."

"You love it and you know it." They ate in companionable silence for a whole two minutes.

"So," Stacy dragged out the word.

Megan knew it was just a matter of time before Stacy asked, and before Megan told all. It was a friend thing.

"Has he really never sent a woman flowers?" She touched a finger to a delicate blossom, her heart picking up its beat.

Stacy raised a hand. "I swear on his grave, which will be soon if he's hurt you. Mom even had to buy prom corsages because he said it was a waste of money. He'd opt for a milkshake after the dance."

She laid a hand on Megan's. "Did he hurt you? I know secrets I can tell the newspaper."

Mega couldn't help but laugh. "You could know where the bodies are buried and you wouldn't turn your brother in."

"It was only the cat," Stacy said with a shrug. "And you were there."

"Why can't life be that simple anymore," Megan sighed, remembering the solemn ceremony the four of them had when the family cat had died.

"Sometimes it can, if you get a different perspective." Her friend came back with the coffee pot.

"Is that a hint?"

Stacy just shrugged. "You don't have to tell me but I know my brother. I've never seen him act the way he does around you. You two have something special, and I'd hate to see it fall apart."

"But if he can't believe in me, or believe with me," Megan started.

"About?" Stacy queried.

"About the ghost," Megan answered matter of fact.

Stacy looked surprised, but only for a moment. "You've seen her? We always thought she was just our imaginations." She paused, then added, "Or maybe you didn't?"

"Well, I didn't realize at first that I was seeing her, or sensing her presence anyway."

"And you never said anything?" Stacy accepted Megan's story without question.

"It's not easy talking about things that make you sound crazy."

"But we're friends. If it's crazy, I'm right there with you. I love the idea of a ghost here. Have you seen her lately?"

Megan told Stacy about the dreams, the green haze, and finally about the spilled drink.

"Wow. She does seem to be trying to make a point. I wonder why nothing has occurred in all the time we've lived here."

"I used to have dreams but they quit when I left for college. Now that I'm back, apparently so is she."

"So it must have something to do with you," Stacy said and Megan wasn't at all sure she liked the idea.

"If that's the case, what do I do about her?"

Stacy shrugged. "From what you've said, she doesn't seem to do any harm. What do you think she wants?"

Megan shook her head. "At this point, I have no idea. That's not the crux of the matter, anyway. Cal said I was being stupid."

"No!" Stacy's eyes widened.

"Well, something to that effect, anyway."

"That is an adjective totally reserved for men."

Megan's phone pinged, but this time it was Harold. When she read the text, she frowned. "I need to get to work. Regardless of where Cal and I are personally, I did tell him I would help on the case."

Stacy reached over and squeezed her hand before getting up. "You'll work it out. You are very special, and my brother, though a total pig at times, does have a heart of gold."

Megan knew it wasn't just sibling loyalty talking. Cal was a good man, just a little hard-headed at times. She bent to draw in a fragrant breath of flowers, smiled, and went in search of her computer.

* * *

Cal wondered how long he should stay away before groveling at Megan's feet. And he would grovel, he had no doubt. His brains had been in his pants the other night or he would have never said what he had.

She had been totally right. If he loved her, and he had come to that awful conclusion when she walked out on him, he had to accept her in all ways. It was just hard to wrap his cop's brain around the idea of a ghost.

Backing up, he decided that loving Megan wasn't awful. The awful part was that since he had never been in love before, he wasn't sure how to proceed. He wasn't given to theatrics like his brother, Jeff, and his analytical brain worked with facts and statistics. Quoting the number of marriages a year or how many lasted more than fifty years was not exactly the romantic lingo a woman wanted to hear.

Should he just pretend nothing was wrong? He sat in his parked truck behind the house pondering his dilemma. Should he give her more time? He looked down at his phone, to the text from Harold, and knew there wasn't more time. He had a case to solve and he could only hope she had made progress on the game. He sucked in a deep breath and opened the door.

She looked up, startled when he came in. Then a mask descended and she spoke in a civil, if slightly cool, voice. "You must have gotten the text from Harold, too."

He slid into the booth across from her, pushed her open laptop aside, and took her hands. He could feel them tremble.

"In a minute. First I want to say I'm sorry."

She blinked, biting her bottom lip. "That's okay," she started, but he wasn't done.

"No, it's not. I should have never discounted your thoughts, or your words. And especially not your feelings." He raised her hands to his lips, kissing her fingers.

"Ah-h-h." Stacy stood by the open kitchen door.

Cal glowered.

"Sorry," she giggled, stepping back and closing both top and bottom sections.

He looked back to see Megan fighting a smile. He shook his head in resignation. "See why I like the boat?"

"It's family. There's no getting away from them."

"Anyway," Cal got his thoughts back on track. "I'm not making excuses, but as a cop, my brain deals with facts and evidence, and occasionally a hypothesis based on those. It's very hard for me to deal with things I can't touch and see."

"Like a computer simulation?"

"Well, that too. I'm not much for fantasy."

She gave him the smile that melted his insides and turned him hard at the same time.

"Oh, I don't know. You gave me a pretty good fantasy a few weeks ago."

"Which I'd be happy to repeat at any time," he said as his phone rang, "except I guess it will have to wait." He punched a button. "Garrett."

"Detective, it's Harold. You didn't answer my text. Can we talk?"

"Not on the phone," Cal said. "We'll come to you."

Megan was already sliding out of the kitchen nook. He rose quickly to block her exit, capturing her waist and drawing her close to softly kiss her.

"I *am* sorry," he said, putting his forehead against hers. "And I do want to listen to what you have to say, but can we put Laurie aside for the time being?"

Megan smiled. "She's been hanging around for over two hundred years. I doubt she's going anywhere soon."

Chapter 11

Cal didn't care for going to Porchello every time something came up. He preferred working on his own turf. But the boys didn't have transportation, and he didn't do things over the phone if he could help it. He liked to look someone in the eyes when questioning them.

While he didn't think these guys had anything to do with Dough's death, they did look uneasy, he thought when he and Megan walked into the pancake house. They had picked a different booth, although still in the back, and this time potted plants sat along the top of the bench seats, further obscuring them from view.

Cal just shook his head as he slid into the booth after Megan. Everyone wanted to play detective.

"What's up, fellas?" he asked.

"Why don't we order breakfast first?" Megan said with a smile. The woman could drive him crazy with that smile, but then she added the pat to his leg. He reached beneath the table and twined his fingers with hers.

"It's lunchtime," he said.

"But their strawberry, banana pancakes are the best." She passed the waitress her menu as she ordered.

Cal and the boys opted for lunch. As soon as the waitress disappeared with their orders, he scrutinized the three sitting across from them. Something was definitely going on. Harold, always meticulous, looked like he had slept in his clothes. None of them had shaved, and all could use a haircut.

"You guys been out partying?" he asked with a raised brow.

"Someone's missing," Harold hissed and the other two nodded rapidly in agreement.

Cal's stomach clenched. "Missing?"

They nodded again. Richard looked at Megan and asked, "Did you check her out like we asked?"

Cal turned toward Megan. "You four been talking behind my back?" He was only half teasing.

Megan *tsked* him. "Only in the game. But to answer Richard's question, yes, I located *Comedian2*. She's rather aggressive and rude, but other than that—"

"Wait a minute," Cal interrupted. "How do you know it's a she?"

Megan opened her mouth, shut it and looked at him with amusement. She swallowed, glanced over at the boys, then leaned close to whisper, "Well, see, there are boy shaped avatars and girl shaped avatars."

She was laughing at him, but when he looked across the table, the boys had their heads down, studiously eating French fries. He had left the game up to her, and since he knew nothing about it at this point, he deserved the joke. It still rankled.

"Okay, so who's missing?"

"*Comedian2*," Tom said.

"Wait a minute. Megan just said she's playing aggressively. If she's online, how can she be missing?"

Harold wiped his mouth with his napkin before speaking. "We've been running into her off and on since the game began, so we know how she plays. A couple of weeks ago, she was off-line for almost twenty-four hours. The rules state if you're not online at least once during a twenty-four-hour period, your avatar is deactivated and you have to start over. You lose any treasure you've found and you have to change your location."

"I don't get the connection," Cal said. "Just because she took a nap...?"

"She came back on line, but ever since that time, her game has changed," Tom stated. "Before she wasn't aggressive. It was almost as if she were in the game but really had no interest. Like it was just...a game."

109

No shit, Cal thought. "Megan?"

"I wasn't in the game weeks ago, so I don't know how she played before."

He looked across the table. "So she's on line, but you're saying she's missing?"

"I think it's more," Harold dropped his voice to a whisper. "I think someone else is playing as Comedian2."

"They would have to have her password," Megan said, "and I can't see anyone giving up their password."

"Unless she was threatened, or it was beaten out of her," Cal said under his breath. "You did say there was a pretty hefty prize for the winner of this game, didn't you?"

Richard nodded. "A quarter of a million."

Cal shook his head. "I don't understand why people would rather do online gaming and blogging than have an actual conversation with a real person."

"There are maniacs out there, man," exclaimed Tom. "It's not safe."

Cal looked from one face to the next. They were serious.

"Like this is? You have no idea who's out there in this fantasy world of yours; how many psychos there are."

"It's not fantasy," protested Richard. "That's like *World of Warcraft*."

Cal exploded. "It's fucking fantasy," he hissed, "except that one person is dead and another might be missing. *That's* pretty real."

"Excuse me," Megan said, bumping against Cal. "I have to use the restroom."

Cal automatically slid out of the booth, but instead of going past him, Meg stood with her back to the boys and looked him right in the eyes.

"Bullying isn't going to work here," she said softly.

"Can we stop the game? Get all the players together?"

"You probably could find a way to do that," she said, "but if it's someone within the game, that would defeat the purpose."

Cal glanced over her shoulder to the boys. "If they keep playing, how can I guarantee their safety?"

110

She gave him a quick kiss on the cheek. "You'll find a way."

Cal watched her go, gave a sigh, and sat back down.

"There's something else, Detective," Tom said.

"Christ, what now?"

"I think, but can't confirm, that *Comedian2* treasure is the Bahia Emerald."

Harold and Richard were shaking their heads. "She can't use that, Tom," Harold said. "It has to be an obscure, undiscovered treasure and the Emerald has been all over the news."

"So someone might think she really has this emerald." Cal followed Tom's train of thought. "Someone might have gotten a hold of her and/or has taken her place in the game to find it?"

Harold stated again, "That's not following the rules."

"Harry, in case you haven't figured it out yet, someone is already breaking the rules."

"It's going to storm," Megan said, as she slipped back into the booth. "Do you guys need a ride back?" Thunder rumbled in the distance.

"No, our hotel is close," Richard said.

His comment brought up another question for Cal. "You said you were all here for spring break, but that was over weeks ago. How are you managing to still be here?"

"We decided to stay and keep at the game together."

"No jobs; school to go back to?" Cal had never had the opportunity to while away his life. Actually, he would have never thought to do so.

"Harold and I have graduated," Richard said as everyone stood, "so we spend some time on line job hunting. Tom's doing online grad work so all he needs is a computer."

Cal dropped some bills on the table. "All right. Same rules this time. Don't talk to anyone about this and let me know if anything shows up on the message board. I'll do some checking on our missing person, but frankly, that's a crap shoot. People go missing every day from just about every city in the country."

"And the emerald?" Tom asked.

"Emerald?" Megan parroted.

"Later," he said to her as more thunder rolled and a streak of lightning flashed right outside the window. He pushed her toward the entrance.

* * *

They got to the truck just as the rain started, but Cal sat, staring out the window. Megan followed his line of sight and watched as the boys hurried down the street and turned at the entrance of one of the upscale resorts in the area.

Only when they disappeared did he start the truck and pull out of the parking lot. "At least they're not in some rat shack," he grumbled. Thunder boomed as though in agreement.

The sky had turned dark with massive clouds rapidly scurrying overhead. Huge raindrops hit the window and Megan thought she heard some hail along with it. It came so quickly and so heavy that she couldn't see further than the front of the truck and she wondered how Cal was managing. She glanced his way and decided not to say anything that would break his concentration.

Traffic slowed to a crawl as they got into town. When a car coming from the opposite direction sprayed a wall of water over the truck, Cal swore but kept moving slowly forward.

It wasn't until they stopped that she realized they were at his condo complex, parked under the small portico at the front entrance. The overhang blocked most of the rain.

"I doubt I have to get you home for a tour now," he said.

"Actually, I didn't have anything scheduled." She gave him a smile.

"Good. Then I don't have to worry about getting you home at all."

Megan's heart pounded.

He separated his keys and gave her one ring. "Go in this way. I have to park out back and there's no cover. No sense both of us getting wet."

Megan grabbed her computer, which she had taken but not used this time, and shoved it up under her shirt.

Cal groaned.

"What? I don't want it to get wet and the rain's coming sideways."

"I just don't think I've ever envied a computer before." He leaned across and tapped it through her shirt. "Get rid of it before I get in because no way in hell are you going to be using it tonight."

Megan was surprised her legs supported her as she jumped down and hurried to the door. She tried three keys before she found the one that opened the secured entrance. She fumbled again at the condo door. It wasn't as though she didn't know what was coming, but that was exactly why she was nervous. Cal had a way of making her ache in places she hadn't known existed.

Dropping her computer on the couch, she dashed to the bathroom for towels, wrapping one around her hair and getting back to the door with the other just as Cal came in.

"You're soaked," she exclaimed, tossing him the towel. "Stay on the rug and strip."

He peeked out from beneath the towel as he rubbed his hair. "Now there's a statement a guy likes to hear." He paused, staring, and Megan looked down. Her own shirt was wet, the thin material almost transparent.

"Care to join me?" Cal asked with a grin.

"I'm not dripping," she replied.

"So?" He shucked his shirt and toed out of his shoes. His socks plopped as he dropped them on the floor. His hands paused at his belt and he looked at her, his silver gaze intent.

"Well?" The belt slicked through the wet cloth and dropped to the pile.

Megan pursed her lips to keep from smiling. Regardless, her tongue slipped out and she licked her lips. Cal's gaze narrowed.

"I'm rather enjoying the show." She tipped her head to one side, her gaze taking in the broad expanse of his chest and the narrow vee of dark hair pointing downward until it disappeared beneath the waist of his trousers. She could see where the pants bulged, and because she knew exactly what was beneath, she sauntered over.

"Perhaps I can help," she said, replacing his hands on the zipper.

"Perhaps I can help you catch up," Cal whispered hoarsely as he slipped off her shirt and unhooked her bra in a single movement. What started out slow and seductive grew frenzied as they both tugged and pulled at their remaining clothes. Thunder crashed and lightning brightened the dim interior as if telling them to hurry.

The minute they were naked, Cal pulled her close and kissed her with a silent urgency that skittered across her nerves and pooled low in her belly. His hands were everywhere, caressing her back, sliding down her hips, then suddenly stopping high along the inside of her thighs. His thumbs separated her, rubbing across her clit. Her hips jerked.

"Cal."

"Sh." The sound whispered across her skin as he kissed her everywhere, stopping momentarily to nip her nipples before kneeling in front of her. He sucked the sensitive skin on her hip, trailed his hot tongue down her thigh and then back up, so slowly she thought she would die. She grabbed his hair, hoping to direct him and she could feel his smile against her skin.

When his mouth replaced his hands, she shrieked, and her knees would have buckled if he hadn't grabbed her thighs to hold her close.

"Oh, god," she moaned and that quickly, her body broke into a million pieces as shimmers shot through her. Her insides clutched when he slid a finger in, touching that secret place that kept her at a peak. He barely pushed, and she went over the edge again.

"Sweet," Cal said as he kissed his way back up her midriff. He stopped again at her breasts, molding them with his large hands, caressing until her nipples peaked.

"You are so sweet." He ran his fingers through her hair, pulling it back from her face.

Megan had never had a man look at her the way Cal did at that moment. She couldn't put words to it; just feelings such as wonder and joy. And then he did what no man had ever done before. He tucked an arm behind her knees and picked her up, cradling her against his chest.

She squealed. "Stop. You can't lift me." But she wrapped her arms around his neck anyway.

"I can," he said, tickling her ear with his tongue. "I am," he added as he walked down the hall to his room and kicked the door closed behind them. "I did." With that, he dropped her onto the bed and fell in beside her.

"You are my hero," she rolled toward him, batting her eyelashes before bending down for a kiss, which started slowly but escalated rapidly, just as things did every time they touched. The rain was so heavy it obscured the afternoon sun, but she didn't need light to read Cal's body. Just as she had, his muscles quivered beneath her touch, and when she circled him, all she heard was a sharp hiss as he sucked in his breath. But it wasn't enough.

"Something you probably didn't count on," she whispered, leaning forward so her breasts rubbed against his chest.

"What?" The word was a breath of sound as he lifted his hips, urging her on.

"I like being in control." She slid her hands up and circled his wrists, pinning them to the mattress near his head. She leaned close, but when he lifted his head to capture a breast, she moved back and grinned.

"My turn," she said as she slid a leg over, straddling his waist.

She knew he could easily break her grip, but all he said was, "And?"

She scooted back, lifting her hips. "I like it hard and fast."

As quick as the lightning flashing outside, Megan found herself on her back, a rough-haired leg thrown over hers, and her own wrists now captured in his large hands.

When she raised her gaze from his heaving chest to his narrowed eyes, it was to find him slowly shaking his head.

"I work hard, I drive fast and can shoot a gun even faster." He bent to trace the swell of her breast with his hot tongue. "But baby, lovemaking is meant to be slow." He gently nipped her nipple. "Incredibly slow and combustible."

As he spoke, he just barely entered her; stopped, then pushed in a little more. She closed her eyes with a sigh.

"Look at me." He kissed her nose. When she raised her gaze to his, she saw his heart in his eyes; everything she had ever wanted lay before her. And even though he didn't say the words, she knew he was hers, forever.

She raised her hips, opening to him, but he pulled back. When she pouted, he gave her a little more, inch by inch, each time pulling out to the very edge before slowly – *god, so slowly* – pushing back in. When he had filled her completely and her muscles squeezed around him, he went still. She didn't know if it was the thunder outside or her heartbeat, but the sound roared as he finally began to move; as he set about proving that slow was indeed better than fast. As for hard, it was soon replaced with multiple.

* * *

Megan woke, for a moment disoriented until she felt Cal's arm draped casually across her hips. She felt the warmth of his chest against her back, heard his breathing, slow and soft. He had not awakened her, although she knew if she moved her hips back just slightly, she would most surely awaken him.

Something else had intruded on her sleep. The room was in shadow; mid-day darkened to twilight. She heard thunder rumble in the distance, but it was another sound that had awakened her. She sneaked out from beneath Cal's arm and snagged a shirt he had left tossed on a chair. As

116

she buttoned it, she moved to the balcony doors, peering out. At that moment, the heavens opened again and rain came down, this time in a straight, soft, and silent curtain.

She opened the door and stepped out onto the balcony, protected by a small overhang. Off to the west it was already lighter but she wished it would remain dark with the clouds, the rain and a heaviness to the air that wrapped around her. She loved thunderstorms, especially in the middle of the day. They were mysterious, and made her feel like something unknown was still to come as the air cooled and sounds became more vibrant.

It always rained in mysteries she read. The heroes usually had to traverse swollen streams and torrential downpours to rescue their fair ladies from disaster. She looked back to the bed, where Cal now laid sprawled on his back, arms overhead, with the sheet just barely covering his hips.

"He is your hero, just as Logan was mine."

Megan clamped a hand across her mouth to keep her scream inside. Her heart pounded in her chest as she looked rapidly around, not really expecting to see her, but there, in the corner of the balcony, stood Laurie.

There was no doubt in Megan's mind that's who it was. She wore a dress similar to the ones Megan herself wore for the tours. Her fair hair was long, falling almost to her waist, and her hands were clasped in front of her. But it was her face that cemented the fact Megan was seeing a ghost. Pale skin, eyes that almost glowed, and an aura of blue surrounding her.

Behind her, the sky was a contradiction, the high dark clouds edged in light as the sun tried unsuccessfully to break through. Lower wisps of gray sped north with the wind, boldly proclaiming more rain as a gray haze built on the horizon. When bits of sun broke through, making raindrops glitter, Laurie looked almost transparent.

"What do you want from me?" Megan whispered.

"The river is rising and there are traitors among us. You must beware." Her voice had a sing-song quality that held Megan mesmerized.

A streak of lightning, followed instantly with the crash of thunder, caused Megan to jump and quickly shut her eyes. When she opened them, the vision was gone.

"What's going on?"

This time, Megan did squeal as arms came around her from the back. She began shaking and his arms tightened.

"You're cold. Why are you out here in the rain?" Cal nuzzled her neck, his breath warm on her skin.

The sun peaked from behind a cloud; the rain drizzled to a stop and only a soft grumble could be heard. She felt an incredible sadness, and wasn't sure if it was because Laurie was gone, or because the storm was over. She wanted neither to end so soon. She longed to remain wrapped in the storm and the past, because she knew in the present that Cal was going to want answers.

"She was here," she said before he could question her.

"Come back to bed." Cal took her hand and led her inside, shutting the door and closing the drapes now that the sun was out.

Megan stopped by the bed, pulling her hand from his. "You don't believe me."

Cal sighed. He didn't look at her as he undid the shirt she wore; slowly, one button at a time.

"I believe in things I can see – family, sorrow, happiness," he said softly as he let his hands slide down her arms with the shirt. "Beauty," he added as he cupped her breasts, bending to kiss them gently.

Megan shivered at his touch, longing to forget everything else but the feelings he evoked with simply his gaze. But this was too important.

"But not ghosts?"

He did look at her then. "There's a lot I can't see that I have to take on faith. I guess this is one of them."

"Why?" He was doing incredible things with his hands and Megan was losing her train of thought.

His mouth came to hers in a kiss so sweet, so gentle, Megan could have melted into a puddle at his feet. She forgot everything as he explored, igniting her senses, his tongue darting out to mimic the movement of his hips.

"Why?" he asked as his hands cradled her face. "Because I love you, Megan, and therefore I believe in you."

She tried not to cry, but hot tears ran silently down her cheeks. Cal lifted her and gently laid her on the bed, coming down on top. He kissed away her tears and when she opened her legs to welcome him, they came together in an unspoken promise – to love, and to believe.

Chapter 12

"So, tell me about Laurie." Cal's voice sounded casual, but Megan could feel his chest still heaving, just as hers was.

She gave a shaky laugh. "This is your idea of romantic, post-climactic conversation?" She continued stroking his chest.

"Climaxes," he emphasized the plural.

"Mmm," Megan murmured, content to just lie there.

"Megan?"

She began to wiggle uncomfortably. He had said he believed her. He had even said he loved her, but was she ready to put that to the test? To give herself a bit of time, she scooted up against the headboard, wrapping the sheet over her breasts.

"A little late for modestly, isn't it?" He turned, bracing himself on an elbow, his gloriously nude body in repose, but definitely still very masculine.

Megan chewed her lip, debating what to tell him. Then she mentally laughed. They had made love half the night, exploring each other's bodies until she knew exactly where he was ticklish and he had discovered the tiny birthmark on the underside of her breast. And let's not forget the small tattoo high on his bicep, the word *family* surrounded by a heart. That really said it all. Yet she didn't want to talk about a silly ghost?

He grabbed the sheet at her breasts, tugging. "If you don't want to talk, I can think of other things to do."

"Stop." She pulled the sheet back up. As much as she loved *making love* with Cal, her body still tingled from the last bout and she just couldn't do it again.

"Okay, if you want to play hardball." Cal lowered his brows, frowned, and said in an I-can-get-information-out-of-you BPD detective voice, complete with thick Boston accent. "Have you actually seen the suspect? Has she spoken to you, given you any indication of what she wants? What does a woman look like who's over two hundred years old?"

She laughed. "Yes, yes, pretty."

Cal frowned for real. "Let's take it from the top."

She swatted his bare chest. "If you stop playing detective."

He scooted up beside her and wrapped an arm around her bare shoulders. "All right. Just tell me what you've seen and heard. You said she was here tonight?"

Megan nodded. "This was the first time I'd actually seen her as a person. The other times, there has just been a green haze. And she looks just like I imagine she did when she died – young, very pretty, and dressed in clothes from that time period."

"From the beginning," he said, his eyes closed in concentration.

"First just a green haze, then an icy touch and whispered 'you can help'." She looked at him and gasped. "There was that spilled beer, too. I'm sure that was her."

He opened one eye to look at her. "What did she say tonight?"

"That the river was rising and there were traitors among us; to beware. Then she vanished."

"Isn't there something in the tour script about the churning river that night? I know there's something about betrayal."

"Are you saying I'm just projecting?" She sat up straight.

"No." He pulled her back against him. "I'm analyzing." At her look, he added, "That's what detectives do. First, it seems that your Laurie is getting bolder – appearing more often, manifesting enough to actually do something and now finally showing herself and speaking with you. Secondly, she seems to be sending you a message."

"But what does it all mean?"

"I'm not sure of that. It takes a lot of energy for a ghost to physically move something, become visible or to speak. It drains them and they have to lie low for a time to recharge. So you may not see her for a while."

He was spouting information like an authority. "And you know this how?"

His cheeks grew ruddy and he looked everywhere but at her. She found that one sensitive spot and tickled. He grabbed her and rolled over, pinning her beneath him.

"Okay, so I did some research."

If she didn't already love him, she would have fallen hard in that second. "You don't believe in ghosts."

"What can I say? I'm a sucker for a pretty face."

* * *

Cal decided as he made breakfast the next morning that being in love made a man a total sap. Not only had he actually *told* Megan he loved her, but he had told her about his research. The only scrap of self-esteem he had left was that he hadn't told her he had started his research after the very first time she had mentioned the ghost.

An acquaintance of his through work, who was now a professor of psychology at Harvard, also belonged to the Association for the Scientific Study of Anomalous Phenomena. Cal had always laughed at Keith's beliefs in the paranormal, yet he was the first person Cal had called. Keith was duly excited about the idea of an actual haunting in Boston, because according to him, there were very few ghosts actually documented. Keith said he would go on the tour one night when Megan was narrating, as that seemed the only time the specter appeared. Now, Cal would have to call him and try to explain this latest happening.

"Good morning."

Cal actually jumped at the sound, turning quickly to where Megan stood, framed in soft sunlight that filtered in through the kitchen window. It highlighted her hair with streaks of gold and made the oversized shirt she wore practically transparent. He had to ask himself how he deserved such a beautiful, wonderful woman.

"Penny for your thoughts," she said, coming close to wrap her arms around his waist in a hug.

"I'm thinking I should turn off the stove and take you back to bed."

"My, my. Aren't we lecherous this morning? If we did that, I wouldn't get to sample your..." she looked over his shoulder, "French toast? You're making me French toast?" She squeezed him harder. "You are amazing!"

"Because I can cook?" He paused before adding, "Is that all?" Her arms and warmth left him and he turned to see her reaching up into the cupboard for a coffee mug. He whistled softly as her bare butt was exposed.

She came back to him with the empty cup, setting it on the counter near the stove. She cupped his face with both hands and gave him a kiss hotter than the griddle.

"You were absolutely amazing last night." She kissed him again. "And this morning. Not that I think your ego needs any boost. Besides, I think I contributed my fair share." She stepped back. "You're burning my breakfast."

"Damn." Cal shuffled the pieces of toast off the griddle onto plates as Megan laughed. The happy sound settled inside him, warming him in a way that even their lovemaking hadn't. He could get very used to hearing that sound every day of his life.

"Grab the syrup," he said as she nosed through the fridge for cream for her coffee. Together they sat at the table and ate in companionable silence.

He sighed over the last of his coffee. "I need to shower and get to work." But he sat there in contemplation.

"I should get on line before I head home," she said, unwinding from the chair but he snagged her as she went past and hauled her onto his lap.

"Why does life have to interfere with...life," he whispered as he kissed the exposed skin where his shirt drooped off her shoulder. His hand slid up her bare leg and nudged between her thighs, searching out her secrets. "If I owned the crown jewels, I'd give them up in a heartbeat to plunder your treasures."

She jerked upright, squeezing her legs together. "Jewels; treasure?" Jumping off his lap, she hurried into the living room and reappeared with her laptop. She spoke as she opened the screen and began typing. "What was it Harold said yesterday about *Comedian2's* treasure?"

Cal shrugged. "Something about an emerald that was real, not just an obscure artifact. Not that it makes any difference. The real problem is trying to trace someone they think is missing when we have no clue as to where to start."

He looked over, but Megan appeared lost in thought, the light from the computer screen reflecting in her gaze.

Ping.

He watched her read whatever had popped up.

"Tom says he's tried to communicate with *Comedian2* and gets no reply. Apparently she's playing, but he says before she's talked to him and now she doesn't."

Ping.

This time she frowned as she read.

"What is it?" he asked, getting up to stand behind her. He bent forward to view the message.

"*DragonFyre: I know where you are. I'm coming for you.* What the hell does that mean?"

Megan shook her head. "It's just one of the players, although I haven't come across him before."

Ping.

"Be careful, Harold says. *DragonFyre* is asking really pointed questions," Megan read him the text, even as she fired off a reply.

"If we could only get in touch with the game creator; get the names and locations of the players," Cal mused. "Or better yet, get him to shut down the game."

She turned to him. "I believe whoever masterminded this game is the same person who is behind John Dough's murder and maybe this missing person."

"Why do you think that?"

"From the very fact that there *are* no messages on the board. There was no message when John Dough died, and there's been no message about a missing player. Why wouldn't the creator say something; caution people, if he were not somehow involved? Why wouldn't he come forward?"

Cal's heart twisted and his breathing caught. "You need to get out of the game." His fingers tightened on her shoulders.

"Why?"

"Are you kidding me? If what you say is true, you could be in danger."

"We don't *know* that it's true; it's just conjecture. Maybe the creator doesn't know what happened to Dough. We have no idea where he's located."

Cal scrubbed his hands over his face. What a tangled mess. Megan's phone chirped and she picked it up.

"Hey, Jeff. What's up? Yeah, all right. I can do that." She hung up and went back to the computer screen.

"What'd he want?" Cal asked as if he didn't know.

"Andrea has a doctor appointment and he wanted to know if I could do a downtown tour this afternoon."

"What if I had something planned?" He turned her chair around so she faced him. Gripping the arms on both sides, he pinned her in, very slowly lowering his mouth to hers.

"You have to work," she said then ran her tongue around her lips and wiggled it at him.

With a growl, he swooped in for a kiss, all fire and heat and dueling tongues. She looped her arms around his neck and he lifted her, wrapping her legs around his waist.

Without taking his mouth from hers, he managed to get a hand beneath her bottom and jerked his sweatpants down.

In two long steps, he pinned her against the wall and took her in one sensuous stroke. She gasped; he groaned. She bit his neck; he rammed harder. This time it wasn't slow. This time he was demanding, but she gave it right back, squeezing him with her thighs and with her sweet, wet heat.

"I can't," he managed to gasp, knowing he would come any second and feeling selfish. He felt her inner muscles tighten.

"Right there with you," she said as she bit him again.

It was over too soon. He leaned his forehead against hers, sucking in deep gulps of air. His hands shook on her fanny; his arm muscles quivered.

"Wow," she breathed the single word, her breath hot against his neck as she slowly unwound her legs and dropped her feet to the floor.

"Yeah. You okay?"

Her smile could have lit up the city. "Definitely okay."

They stood together for a few minutes. He caressed her back and she returned the favor, lightly scratching up and down his spine with her nails. He kissed along her hairline, perfectly content.

"I really do need to get to work," he finally said without much conviction, Megan was happy to note.

"Yeah, you really do." She didn't dare kiss him again. He made her ravenous, even after what they had just done she couldn't get enough of him. She knew that wasn't fair to him because there were things that needed to be done. That didn't make the yearning in her body any the less.

She watched as he walked away, his back a wide stretch of bronze muscle she longed to reach out and caress again. He reached up to rub his fingers through his hair and she smiled. He really did need a haircut.

While he showered, she sent feelers out, playing the game, and texted Harold about the emerald since Cal had not said anything more about it. He had just answered when

Cal came out of the back room, trousers hanging loose on his hips as he pulled a polo shirt over his head.

"Holy shit, Garrett," she hollered at him when she read Harold's text.

His head popped out, his hair sticking out in wild but sensuous disarray. "What?"

"You didn't tell me it was the *Bahia* Emerald. How could you not tell me that?"

He shrugged, sitting in the chair next to her and pulling on a sock. Before he had a chance to say anything, she turned her laptop around so he could see the page she had opened. He glanced at it while pulling on his other sock.

"Never mind," she said, turning it back. "I'll give you the highlights. I heard about the Bahia when I was in LA. It is an actual huge chunk of emerald, originally mined in Brazil and said to be worth over four hundred *million* dollars."

"Well, shit," Cal said with a resigned sigh. "So now we're talking a little more than the quarter of a million prize money."

"The thing is, *Comedian2* couldn't actually own it. Reviewing the articles found about it, there are all kinds of controversy about ownership and it's supposedly being kept in safe storage by the L. A. sheriff." She looked back at the screen. "Hmm."

"What are you thinking?"

"Maybe *Comedian2* has some connection with one of the reported owners, so she decided to use it as her treasure, simply because she knew about it and didn't have to research for something different."

"If it's in LA, that narrows down the search for a missing person," Cal said as he rose, tucking his shirt into his trousers and zipping them up.

"Maybe and maybe not," Megan replied. "The Bahia has been shuffled around, lost and found, claimed and reclaimed for some time. *Comedian2* might be from one of the other places the emerald has been."

"Give me the places. That's still got to be less than searching the entire country."

"LA, Las Vegas, New Orleans, San Jose, Idaho," she said as she wrote them down.

"Idaho?" He scanned the paper, his brow furrowed. "Thanks." He kissed her, almost absently, and she knew his mind was already at work.

"Later," he said, just as the door clicked shut behind him.

Megan sat, staring at the door. "What just happened?" she asked herself before she started to giggle. It was like they were an old married couple – just a quick kiss and a hasty good-bye as they passed each other and hurried on about their business. That sounded rather boring and she wasn't at all sure she wanted that for the rest of her life.

However, she easily recalled last night's marathon and this morning's interlude against the dining room wall. She shook her head as she went to get a second cup of coffee. Whatever the future held for her and Cal, she knew it wouldn't be boring.

Chapter 13

You would think people would stare, Megan thought later as she rode the subway down to the Commons. Her green, flower sprigged dress brushed the floor, hiding her sneakers, which were the only modern thing on her. One hand grasped the ribbons of her bonnet and the other a small wicker basket, the equivalent of a purse for the era she was portraying. Her hair was tucked back into her snood.

When people did glance her way, they simply smiled and nodded, as though seeing a woman in eighteenth century attire were a typically normal occurrence. Which, she supposed, it was for Boston, Massachusetts. Her mind, however, was not on the tour she would be giving in just a bit. As the train swung around a curve and she automatically grabbed a strap above her, she went back over the bits and pieces she had gleaned that morning.

She had stayed at Cal's awhile, playing the game and actually capturing another treasure. Harold and Tom were in awe, sending her congrats texts. A few other players battered at her fortress but she had easily repelled them. Right before she had shut down, *DragonFyre* had returned, this time getting dangerously close to ramming a wall. She managed to block the breach and the avatar had belched fire as he turned away.

The other players in the game had seemed much like Harold, Tom and Richard – gamesters and determined, but good natured and willing to concede when necessary. *DragonFyre* was different – his name was dark; his avatar was even a man with a dragon head that actually spit fire. Everything about him was dark and foreboding, and now that he had begun lurking around her fortress, she felt an unexplainable unease.

The red line screeched to a stop at Park and she got off, walking up the stairs into the sunlight. The afternoon was clear and marginally cool for the end of June. As she walked toward the visitor's center, she tied her bonnet beneath her chin and mentally began to review the tour highlights. While she needed the exercise, she was glad this was one of Jeff's shorter tours and not the entire Freedom Trail. Instead, they would walk around the Boston Common, then up past the Old Granary Burial Ground, on to Faneuil Hall and Quincy Market, and end out at Long Wharf.

Today's group consisted of several families, she noted as she stopped in the shade to one side of the visitor's center entrance. Lots of children; not too many senior citizens. She liked any age group of people, but mixing children with older people often led to complications. For one thing, the elders usually didn't walk as fast as the children wanted to go.

"Are you our guide?" A little boy tugged on her skirt. "What's your name?"

"I am Miss Megan," she said. "What's your name?"

"Logan," he promptly responded.

"Well, hello, Logan. Are you ready to learn some Boston history?"

He nodded. "That guy over there," he pointed, "has already been telling me some stuff. He's lived here all his life." He leaned closer and whispered, "I think he's Benjamin Franklin."

She turned toward where he had pointed. The man did, indeed, look like Franklin, although a much younger version. The top of his head was totally bald with longish hair around the sides and back. His stomach reminded her of Santa Clause, and he wore wire-rimmed glasses perched on the end of his nose. His historic appeal was fractured, however, by his brightly printed Hawaiian shirt, khaki shorts, and black strap sandals with white ankle socks.

129

He was fiddling with some kind of device which hung from a strap around his neck, a small black box like a very old fashioned box camera. Ah, tourists, she smiled, raising her hands to bring everyone together.

"Welcome to Boston," she said. "Are you ready to learn about our history?" As the children yelled *yes,* she turned and set out across the Boston Common. It was going to be a great day.

***

Cal had never been so frustrated in his life. They had entered the five places Megan had given him into the data base, resulting in thousands of hits on missing persons. Even narrowing the search to female didn't decrease the numbers by much, some of them dating back to the nineties.

"Give me only the last three months," he said to Dan, who had been working steadily with him for the past several hours. "No, make that only the last two." According to the boys, this player had only been acting strange for a while, which he hoped meant she hadn't been missing that long.

Bingo. The list on the enlarged screen in front of him was narrowed to about twenty. As he watched, pictures began to pop up as Dan clicked on names to bring up their files. He began scanning the information, hoping something would jump out at him. There was no one from Idaho or New Orleans, so at least that narrowed it down. Of course, he couldn't be sure any of the other locations were correct, but it was a starting place. Otherwise, he had nothing to go on but an online gaming name and an avatar. He couldn't...

Grabbing his phone, he quickly called Megan. When it went right to voice mail, he remembered she was giving a tour. He dialed Harold.

"Can you send me a screen shot of the missing girl's avatar?" he asked the instant Harold answered.

"Well, yeah, if we can find her. She keeps going off line."

"Is that normal?" Cal asked.

130

"Not if you want to win the game," Harold replied. "She stays on just long enough not to get eliminated. And she's still playing weird." There was a pause, then he asked, "Where's Megan?"

Cal's heart rate doubled. "Why? What's wrong?"

"Nothing," Harold hurried to explain. "It's just that we haven't seen her on line for hours and this *DragonFyre* dud is pounding her fortress. We can't form an alliance to help her unless she's online and asks."

Cal's head hurt. The game dynamics were beyond him. He concentrated on what he could actually do. "Do you know anything, anything at all, about this *Comedian2*?"

The line was silent for a minute. "Harold?"

"Sorry. I was just asking the guys. The thing is, everything is supposed to be secret. That's part of the game; not knowing who someone is, you know? But…"

"To hell with game secrets, Harry," he said, knowing the nickname would get the kid's hackles up. "What do you know?"

"Sometimes; not always, but sometimes, a player has some hint who he or she is in their avatar and in their name."

"I figured the avatar might be designed to look like the player," Cal replied. "That's why I need a screen shot."

"Okay. Good," Harold's voice was muffled as though he were holding a hand over the phone. Then it cleared. "Detective, Tom just located *Comedian2* and is sending you an avatar shot."

"What else were you saying? Something about names?"

"Hints. For example, Megan was born in 1987, wasn't she? Thus the number in her name, *Mystic87*. I go by the *Red Baron*, for obvious reasons."

"Obvious?" Cal started then recalled Harold's bright red hair. "Okay. So we need to dissect her name, *Comedian2*?"

"Well, I'm not saying that's what everyone does, but it's a starting point."

"Yeah, thanks, kid," he said and hung up. They had to start somewhere.

* * *

"And here we are at Long Wharf," Megan said as she guided the group across the Rose Kennedy Greenway and into the shade of the Customs House. "If you recall passing Faneuil Hall on State Street, this wharf originally extended from there over a third of a mile into the Harbor, into deep water so that ships could tie directly to the wharf to unload their goods into the warehouses."

"But it's land, not water," one youngster said.

"That's right," Megan replied. "At one time, Faneuil Hall was right on the shoreline and this was all water. Over time, the people of Boston wanted more land, so they reclaimed the shoreline to include areas now occupied by Quincy Market and the Customs House."

She looked around the group. It had been a great tour, with lots of interesting questions. "You're welcome to linger and explore the waterfront. There are restaurants, the Aquarium, and if you go down this way," she pointed "and across the bridge, there's a Children's Museum. Thank you so much for taking an historic Boston Tour with JG Tours." She shook hands with a few of the group; smiled for pictures with others. As soon as the last of her group had wandered off, she removed her bonnet and used it to fan her face.

"You must beware," hissed a voice to her side in the shadows of the building.

Laurie, in her period dress which looked much like the one Megan wore, stood there wringing her hands.

"What are you doing here?" Megan whispered, facing the wall, hoping people wouldn't notice her talking to herself. Because, as solid as Laurie looked, Megan was sure no one else saw her. "You're a river ghost. I mean, that's where you were…that's where I see you."

"You must beware," she said again. She looked around as though lost, wrapping her arms about her waist. "My

132

father's warehouse; Logan. There's danger, from one of your own. I thought I saw Logan." Her words ran together and Megan was trying to decipher them when a hand came down on her shoulder. She jumped, squealed and took a quick step sideways, away from the touch. When she looked back, Laurie was gone.

"You appeared to be talking to someone," said the man on the tour who looked like Ben Franklin. "Are you alright?" The little box around his neck beep-beeped slow and steady and the sound, along with the man's concerned face, steadied her nerves.

"No, I," Megan hesitated. "Do I know you?"

He chuckled. "Probably not that you recall. I was a student when your father was at BU, but I have since moved across the river to Harvard." He put out his hand. "Dr. Keith Farrington."

"Of course. I do remember. My father was always having students over to the house. I think he feared they didn't eat well, so we were always having barbecue and picnics. You and my father used to get into arguments, friendly ones, if I recall. But what about?"

"We had a distinct difference of opinion as to the past he was disturbing with his archeology digs."

"Disturbing?" Megan's brows rose.

The man shrugged slightly. "It's just that he felt artifacts were just pieces of the past, to be dug up and examined, whereas I believe that to disturb the ground where a culture had lived and died was to disturb the very essence of that culture."

"Exactly what do you teach, Dr. Farrington?"

This time he laughed outright. "I teach psychology, but it would be clearer to you if I just said I belong to the ASSAP."

She silently said the letters, the words they stood for becoming clear. "You're a ghost hunter," she whispered. "How on earth could you know?"

"Shall we sit?" He gestured to the benches scattered among the flower beds.

"Definitely." Megan crossed over and sat, putting aside her basket and bonnet. "Did Cal send you?"

"Your friend, who I know as I have assisted at the police department on occasion, is concerned about you."

"Is that a nice way of saying he thinks I'm nuts?"

"No, no, not at all. In fact, he sincerely believes that you believe you see the spirit of a long dead woman."

She narrowed her gaze. "I have a feeling that's not quite the same thing." She then waved away her disappointment. "Did you see who I was talking to, Professor? Do you see ghosts?" She asked him outright.

"I have studied the phenomena for years, dear girl, but have not had the pleasure of an actual sighting. You really spoke to her, here? What did she say?"

"She told me to beware, which is something she's said before."

"In my research, ghosts have a tendency to stay close to where their demise occurred. Why would she follow you here, I wonder?"

Megan was certain it was a rhetorical question, for she hadn't the foggiest idea. "She said she was looking for Logan, her betrothed." She paused in thought. "Oh! There was a little boy on the tour named Logan."

"Purely a coincidence, I'm sure," the professor said. "It's a rather common name. I wonder what else there could be."

"Her father had a warehouse on the wharf," Megan said. "He was a tea merchant, or so the story goes. Logan worked for him."

"Hmm. So perhaps she really was looking for her young man. Interesting." Dr. Farrington stroked his chin in contemplation. "Would you mind, terribly, if I came on the next river tour?"

Megan shrugged. "Jeff is doing it tonight, and he's never said anything about seeing her ghost."

"When might you be doing another?"

"Probably after the weekend. It's the fourth of July, you know, and the city is filled to the brim with tourists celebrating Independence Day. I haven't spoken to Jeff, and I'm sure he's not planning to take any time off." She smiled. "Tourist season is a seven days a week business, it seems."

They stood and he reached into a pocket and pulled out a card, handing it to her. "If you do a tour, I would like to tag along."

Megan shrugged. "You're welcome to come. Perhaps it will keep Laurie from appearing."

"On the contrary. I hope she does make an appearance. Thank you so much, Miss Anderson, for being open and honest with me."

"Megan, please. And it's nice to know I'm not going batty." She shook his hand and he turned to leave. "By the way," she called after him, "the tour is twenty-five dollars a person. I doubt Jeff will give you a pass."

He laughed and waved over his head.

* * *

Megan returned to the house through the back door, hoping to get straight to the basement for a shower and change of clothes, but upon hearing raised voices coming from the front hall, she pushed through the kitchen door into the dining room.

Stacy was standing in the hall, hands on hips, face flushed. "I'm sorry, but I've told you already, we have no rooms available. We're booked for the entire weekend and beyond."

"You must have room. Move your guests together." The man had a heavy accent, one Megan had heard before but couldn't immediately place.

"We don't do that here in Boston," Stacy replied politely, but Megan could hear the strain in her voice. She stepped around the corner, coming up beside her friend.

"May I help?" Perhaps because she was dating a detective or maybe just her own investigative instincts, but Megan studied the man with intensity. He reminded her of Alfred Hitchcock – short and rotund, bald, with beady little eyes. He drew his hands behind his back, squaring his shoulders and she wondered if he thought it made him look more formidable. It only made his stomach more pronounced.

"I demand a room." His gaze flickered from Stacy to her.

She could hear Stacy sputter beside her and reached down to silently clasp her hand in warning. "I'm sure the word *demand* means something totally polite in your native language, so we won't take offense, but as Miss Garrett has already told you, there are no rooms. If you would be so good as to leave, we would appreciate it."

She kept her gaze level, not blinking, hoping that her height and glare would intimidate the man. He continued standing there.

"Stacy, perhaps you would like to call someone?" I said quietly.

"Damn straight," she replied, pulling her phone out of a pocket. "The police." She began to dial and the man actually took a threatening step toward her. Megan started to step in-between when she heard a voice behind her.

"I'm the police. What's going on?" She and Stacy both spun around to see Cal weaving his way around dining room furniture and through the sitting room. Though his arms hung casually at his sides, Megan could tell every instinct was on alert.

"This guy," Stacy started, but when they turned toward the door, it was slamming behind him. "Whew, he's gone."

"What the hell?" Cal said.

"Just an irate tourist wanting a last minute reservation, and on a holiday weekend, too," Stacy said, shrugging off the incident. "It happens once in a while, but usually they're a little more polite about it." She reached up and pecked Cal on the cheek. "Hi there," she said as she slipped around him.

"Megan?" Cal didn't seem satisfied with his sister's explanation.

"What she said, only..." Megan stopped, then gasped. "That's it. I thought there was something about him. He had an accent, just like the man in the Pub that night."

Cal was already past her, grabbing open the front door and pushing the screen wide. She followed more slowly, stopping on the porch as he jumped down the steps and stood on the sidewalk, looking first left then right. Of course the man was nowhere in sight.

"Damn." He gave a frustrated sigh as he came back up the steps. "What did he look like?"

Now that the threat was past, or more likely now that Cal was standing in front of her, large and imposing, and fully armed she was sure, she relaxed. Actually, she began to laugh.

"What's so damned funny?"

"You won't like it," she said.

"Try me."

"The man looked exactly like Alfred Hitchcock."

The silence stretched. He opened his mouth like he wanted to say something, but nothing came out. He rubbed a hand over his face and sighed. "Well, hell."

Curling an arm around her waist, he tugged her along with him as he walked toward the door.

"Have I ever told you how much I like that costume?" He teased as they entered the house. He turned her toward him right inside the door, his hot, hungry mouth descending to devour hers, his large hands spread across her fanny to press her close so she felt his erection through the layers of her petticoats. When he finally raised his head, his eyes glittered; the corners crinkled with humor when he added, "And how much I like getting you out of it?"

Chapter 14

Cal sat in the kitchen with his sister when Megan went downstairs to change. Not that he wanted to, but she had insisted. So he had interrogated his sister.

"How long had that guy been here? Was he alone? Where was he from?"

"Cal, stop." His sister shot him an exasperated look. "Those things happen."

"But you were here alone."

"Which I rarely am," she interjected. "There's always someone around, if not you or Jeff, then a guest, or Matt."

Cal scoffed. "Like Matt could squash a fly." Something about the guy always got on Cal's nerves, and it had taken all his self-control not to run a make on the guy.

"Why are you being so cranky?" she asked. "Is it about your case? You haven't solved it yet?"

"I'm not fricking Superman," he muttered.

"Of course not. You were always Batman and Jeff was Robin." She sat a huge sandwich in front of him and patted his cheek. "I, on the other hand, was Wonder Woman." She emphasized the name as she planted her hands on her hips.

Cal laughed, shaking his head as he grabbed up half the sandwich. His little sister could always put him in a good mood. At the same time, her goodness, and her inherent belief in the goodness of others, often caused him to worry.

"Just be careful, all right?" He questioned around a mouthful of chicken salad.

Megan came in just then and Jeff followed shortly thereafter. From that point, Cal never had a chance to talk to Megan, much less kiss her and do all the kinky things he wanted to do to her. As his family discussed the holiday weekend plans, he sat back and contented himself with watching her, absorbing her smiles and her laugh; the way her green eyes caught the light. She laughed at Jeff's jokes, added her thoughts to Stacy's about the weekend menu, and he realized how right it felt for her to be part of the family. Part of him, really, but therefore a Garrett by extension.

"Mom and Dad are coming in tomorrow," Stacy said as she and Megan cleared the table of chip bowls and empty beer bottles. "You *are* taking the weekend off, aren't you?"

Cal had talked to his dad just the other day, so knew their plans. "I'll be off as long as all the thieves and perverts stay out of my town."

"You're not the only detective in the whole city," his sister said.

"But I'm the best." He wiggled his brows, getting up and pulling Megan to her feet. "See you all tomorrow."

"And we're going where?" Megan asked as he kept her hand in his across the back yard.

"Whoops, wait a minute." He turned and whistled and Jeff popped his head out the door. "You're staying?" Cal asked.

"Yeah, but she'll probably make me sleep on the sofa when she finds out."

"You can have my bed," Megan told him. She looked at Cal. "Apparently I won't need it tonight."

He knew the questions would come the minute they got to his truck. Sure enough, he hadn't even turned the ignition before Megan started.

"Jeff's staying at the house because of that man, isn't he? Do you think he has something to do with our case?"

"I don't know if he has anything to do with anything." He put the truck in gear and backed out.

"Maybe I should have stayed," Megan said.

"Jeff can handle it. Besides, we have other things to do."

"It's late; like what?"

"Like taking a bath—together--in my big tub," he started listing the things he was going to do to her, and

139

before he hit the third stoplight, he wasn't sure he could make it to his condo.

* * *

The holiday weekend was everything Megan remembered from her years with the Garrett family. Although the B&B was full, as soon as breakfast was cleared away, all the tourists were off seeing the sites. At the moment, Cal, Jeff and their dad were outside. She was helping put away the breakfast dishes.

"It is so good to see you again," Sharon, Stacy's mom, said. "You've stayed away far too long."

"I had a good job in L. A. after college."

"I know, but holidays; vacation."

Whereas Cal and Jeff had inherited their dad's dark looks, Sharon was an older version of Stacy with light hair and blue eyes. If not for the additional laugh lines around her eyes and the glasses perched on her nose, Megan thought they could be sisters, rather than mother and daughter. She gave her a hug.

"It was hard, you know," she said, and it had been because everything in Boston reminded her of her parents.

"Uh-oh," Stacy muttered, looking out the side window. "We need to get outside."

She tossed her towel on the counter and headed for the door.

"What's going on?" her mom asked, following in her wake and Megan brought up the rear.

The minute they reached the end of the patio, Megan knew there was trouble ahead. Cal, Jeff, and their dad, Mike, were all pushing on the braces of the gazebo. As they approached, the men moved to the other side and pushed there.

"Stop it," Stacy said, going up to Jeff and smacking his arm. "I didn't tell you to knock it down, just to see if some boards needed replaced."

"They're all loose, honey," her dad said. "It might be easier just to tear it down."

"No," Stacy said. "It's been here forever. Just fix it." Her eyes actually teared up and Megan bit her lip to keep from laughing. His daughter's tears had always been Mike's downfall.

"It hasn't been here *forever*," Cal said. "Wood doesn't last *forever*."

Stacy punched him in the arm, too, but he just laughed, grabbing her around the waist and turning her upside down.

"You want to fight, kiddo?"

"Megan, help!" Stacy shrieked.

Megan was laughing so hard she held her sides. The minute Cal released her, Stacy turned and started after him again, but he quickly dodged behind his mom.

"Honest to Pete," Sharon said as her son used her as a shield, shifting her back and forth by the shoulders. "You're not ten years old anymore."

"She started it," Cal said, giving his mom a quick peck on the cheek.

Megan stood there with tears in her eyes. This was what she had missed all those years in LA, even with those long holiday weekends when her friends would take her with them on their boats, to concerts, to the beach. She had gone, trying to beat the loneliness, but it hadn't been the same. Here, she wasn't an outsider. She was family, or as close to family as she could hope to get.

Always the peacemaker, she spoke up now. "A youngster on my tour said we should compromise if things weren't going our way. Is it possible to shore up the gazebo to get through tourist season, then when it's no longer used as much, it could be rebuilt?"

Mike looked thoughtful. Jeff and Cal walked with him as he more carefully inspected the foundation and the inside cross beams. He pointed. Jeff stood on a bench and reached up under the roof where Megan couldn't see. They stood together in the center, gesturing and pointing, and she heard Sharon sigh; a sigh that echoed Megan's own.

"They are certainly one awesome group of men," Sharon said, "if I do say so myself."

Except for Jeff's long hair, it was hard to tell them apart from this distance. Even at sixty, Mike had his sons' muscular build; bronze skin and black hair that was just beginning to turn silver at the temple.

"You did good, Mrs. G," Megan said, wrapping an arm around her waist in a hug.

"I do despair, though, that neither of them are married yet." She tilted her head slightly as she looked at Megan. "Although I hear there may be hope for at least one of them."

Megan blushed and stammered, but Sharon just laughed.

"Megan Sue, don't you know just how delighted I would be if you became my daughter in truth?"

Megan didn't know what Stacy had told her mom. She knew it probably hadn't been Cal. "It's all very new, you see. Please don't get your hopes up. Things don't always work out."

Sharon linked her arm with Megan's as they walked back toward the patio. "That's where you're wrong, dear. Things always work out as they should."

The rest of that day and most of the next, the men were busy shoring up the gazebo, adding a coat of white paint so it dazzled in the sun. Sharon had gotten out the sewing machine and had new cushions made in no time. Megan busied herself with carting drinks out to the guys, helping Sharon measure and cut, and cooking in preparation for the picnic out on the bay come Monday.

She spent little time online in the game, just enough to keep her avatar active, but did manage to capture a Florida player and the fabled fountain of youth. Tom razed her that she didn't need that particular prize. As soon as she read his text, she deleted it so Cal wouldn't see it. It was just young boy nonsense, but she didn't think Cal would take it that way.

It wasn't until Sunday night as she lay in bed with Cal that there was a chance to catch up.

He groaned as she rubbed Icy Hot across his shoulders and down his arms.

"You didn't need to lift that whole stack of lumber," she reprimanded him, just as she had done when he first pulled the muscle.

"Like I was going to let Dad do it," he grumbled.

"Well, the gazebo looks great, Stacy is happy, and it's done so we can picnic in peace tomorrow."

He rolled over and grabbed her in a bear hug. "How about we skip the picnic and just laze around here all day."

"Not on your life. It's bad enough your folks know I'm staying with you so they can have my room."

"Megan, it's the twenty-first century. Mom's very happy that I hooked up with you."

She leaned back to see him more clearly. "You talked to your mom about us? I thought it was Stacy."

"Of course I talked to her. I've always been able to talk to her about anything." He reached up to kiss her, his hands wandering down her bare back to her fanny, lifting her until she lay on top of him, chest to toe.

"Anything?" She questioned.

"Well, not everything. There are a few things a guy can't tell his mom."

* * *

The fourth of July dawned clear and bright without a cloud in sight and a weather forecast of hot with no chance of rain. When Megan tried to get out of bed, Cal pulled her back in, snuggling her close.

"Don't get up yet," he mumbled into her hair. "It's early, and once we get to the house, I won't have a minute alone with you."

"But your parents are only here for the weekend," she protested, although weakly.

"I lived with my parents for eighteen years. They got plenty of me." He kissed her neck, one hand cupped gently over her breast. "You on the other hand, have only been around for four months."

She laughed. "I lived at your house since I was fourteen."

143

"You were jail bait then." He rolled her over and slid between her legs. "Now," he looked at her with mischief in his gaze. "Now, you're full grown, beautiful, and mine."

He kissed her, long and deep. When he slowly entered her – that agonizingly slow thrust by which he tortured her – she clung to one word; *mine*.

Now, as they drove across town at noon, the sidewalks and streets were bursting with people. Boston was definitely the place to spend Independence Day.

Cal dropped Megan off at the house, said he had an errand, and left.

"I can't believe he's actually taken three days off work," Stacy said when Megan joined her and Sharon in the kitchen. "I bet he's sneaking off now to check in with work." Stacy continued to scoop watermelon out of one half and dropped the chunks into a Tupperware bowl. Megan grabbed a spoon and started on the other half.

"There's no news on the case he has," she said, popping a juicy piece into her mouth. "Oh, wow, that's good!" She ate another before continuing. "I don't know if there's anything else on his plate at the moment, but his phone never rang last night." The instant she said it, she clamped her lips together. She could feel the blush burn her cheeks and neck, clear past the tank top she wore.

"You're definitely good for him," was all Sharon said, but when she looked at Stacy, her friend was grinning from ear to ear. Megan's blush didn't subside as she recalled her conversation with Cal last night. More so for the activity of this morning which she hoped no one ever found out.

"Loading up," Jeff said at the back door. He grabbed the cooler, after checking to make sure there was plenty of beer inside, and carted it outside to the SUV.

"Cal's not back," Megan said as she and Stacy loaded another cooler with food, soft drinks and bottled water.

"Said he'd meet you at the pier," Mike told her. "Don't forget your sunscreen and hats," he said to the room in general as he hefted the picnic basket, grabbed his wife's hand and followed Jeff outside.

"I so love the Fourth of July!" Stacy exclaimed, plopping a sun hat on her head. "It has to be the very best holiday of the whole year."

"What about Christmas; all those presents?" Megan followed her out the back door.

"Okay, so the best holiday of the whole summer." Stacy laughed, tucking her hand in the crook of Megan's arm. "And it's especially great this year because you're back."

They all managed to squeeze into the SUV, packing four into the backseat because Matt showed up as they were loading. Stacy would have sat on his lap but her mom said "seat belts" so they doubled up on the center one, giving Megan little room to breathe.

As they unloaded the SUV onto a pontoon boat in the slip next to Cal's sail boat, he pulled up at the pier. Megan shaded her eyes as not one, but four people spilled out of his truck.

"Who's he got with him?" Stacy asked.

"I'm not sure," Megan replied. It wasn't until they all walked down the ramp to the boat that Megan recognized who was with Cal. When she did, her heart squeezed; actually squeezed so tight in her chest for a moment she thought it had stopped. Then it burst wide open with love.

"Mom, Dad, Jeff, Stacy," Cal said. "This is Tom, Richard and Harold." He put an arm around Megan when she stepped up beside him.

The boys politely shook hands then Mike started directing everyone here and there, issuing orders like a sea captain. Megan turned to Cal, sliding her arms around his waist and hugging him tightly.

"You are such a softy," she whispered as she kissed him, right there in front of everyone.

Cal cleared his throat. "Well, I couldn't see them sitting in their hotel room in Mayberry."

"Of course you couldn't." She smiled through tears.

"But this is real people time, so I made them leave their computers."

"Of course you did." She laughed.

He swatted her on the butt and ordered her aboard. When she turned to reach for one of the dock ties, she noticed that Cal hadn't hopped on deck yet. Instead, he was staring across to where Matt stood, busy texting on his phone. Apparently not everyone had gotten the "no technology" memo.

Cal's dad piloted the pontoon out of the harbor, his family and Matt on board. Cal manned the sailboat, letting the boys and Megan ride with him. He would have rather had Megan to himself but couldn't blame anyone since he had asked the boys to come along.

They were good kids, he thought, as he watched them grin when he yelled "duck" and shifted tack. The boom swung, he tightened the sheet and they zipped across the water. He didn't say anything to Megan, but in route to fetch the boys, he had called work. Just a skeleton staff at the precinct because of the holiday, but Dan had been there, stating no word on any missing person. So all they could do was wait.

He watched Megan lift her hair and loop a band around it, keeping it off her face. The action raised her already perky breasts. Cal stifled a groan. Everything about her turned him on and he couldn't seem to get enough of her. No matter how many times, how long or in what position, he wanted her again and again.

She laughed at something the boys said and it suddenly became clear that it wasn't all about the sex. He liked to hear her laugh. Hell, he liked to *make* her laugh. He realized that he was content just to watch her interact with the people on her tours, the boys on the case, his mom and dad. It was enough to be near her, to wait for her to smile at him like she was now.

Come here, he mouthed, crooking a finger and she came to sit between his legs. He kept one hand on the tiller and the other around her waist as they sailed out of the harbor to Deer Island, where he and his family would picnic and watch the fireworks like they did every year. Only this year, and for all the years to come, he had his very own firecracker.

146

Chapter 15

His angry shouting awakened Megan, who rolled over and began caressing his bare back as he sat on the edge of the bed. She had been reluctant to spend the night, but he had plied her with wine and slow, erotic lovemaking until she said she was too tired to drive home. He hadn't bothered reminding her that she hadn't driven in the first place. He had just carried her off to bed.

Now, as he hollered and in turn listened to the sheriff sputter, her hand slid around his waist to rub his stomach, probably in an effort to calm him down. He stirred against her caress, which only made him angrier since he couldn't do anything about it.

"Protective custody?" he asked, rubbing his forehead where a headache was building. "What the hell does that mean?"

"To protect them," the sheriff said.

"You didn't give them a phone call, did you?" Cal knew the boys would have called him if they had a chance.

"*I'm* calling you for them. Seeing as you and them are so chummy and all." Cal could hear the animosity in the man's voice.

He didn't bother to remind Barney that he had asked for BPD help. It was the sheriff's town, and Cal knew all about being territorial.

"I'll be there as soon as I can." Then he did the unthinkable. "Thank you, Sheriff, for pulling the boys in for protection."

"Cal, what's going on? Did something happen to the boys?" Megan scooted around to sit next to him, peppering him with questions.

He wrapped an arm around her bare shoulders, absently caressing. "Apparently there was a break-in at the hotel -- into the rooms where the guys are staying."

"Oh my God," Megan grabbed his arm. "Were they hurt? We have to go, Cal." She jumped up but he grabbed her hand before she could get away.

"They're all right, Megan. They weren't in their rooms at the time. It must have happened when we were all out on the boat." He glanced at the land line on which the sheriff had reached him. "Why wouldn't they have called me?"

"Damn." He got up, hurrying to the kitchen where he had plugged in his cell last night. Sure enough, there were voice mail messages, timed shortly after he would have dropped them off. "My phone died sometime yesterday, and I plugged it in when we got home, but never bothered looking at it."

"That's not your fault,' Megan said as she poured water into the coffee maker. "They were with us. How could we know something would happen?" She came over to where he stood, still looking at his phone.

"Go get dressed. We'll drink coffee on the way."

They were headed out of town less than twenty minutes later. Cal tried to call Harold but it went right to voice mail. "Protective custody or not, the sheriff must have taken their phones," he mumbled, shutting off his blue tooth.

"Was it a random break in, do you know?" Megan asked. "Were other rooms at the resort broken into? The holidays are bad for that. People know the residents are out sightseeing."

"Barney didn't say. We'll find out." He pulled into the *Deputy Sheriff* slot at the curb parking in front of the sheriff's office.

"Cal?"

"Screw it. We're here on official business." He slammed the truck door and took the steps two at a time.

The receptionist glanced up and was on the phone before he could even say a word. But it was several minutes, of which Cal spent pacing, before the Sheriff managed to show his ass.

"Where are they?" Cal ignored the man's hand when he offered it in greeting.

"Now see here," Barney started.

Megan stepped between them. "Sheriff Barney, I'm Megan Anderson, remember? I'm friends with the young men you have in custody."

"I know who you are," he said. "I checked you out. You're no medical examiner. You're just a reporter, looking for a story, and lady, you're not going to find it in my town."

"Back off," Cal growled. If Barney thought he could intimidate using Megan, he was way off. "This has nothing to do with her."

"Well, I'm not so sure about that," the sheriff said smugly, stuffing his hands in his pockets and rocking back on his heels. "You two have been spending a bit of time in my town, so I was asking myself why."

Cal had known the deputy was tailing them the two times they had visited at the pancake house. He would have probably done the same thing if a murder had gone down in his precinct. That didn't make his anger lessen.

"Let's just see what happened," Megan said in a calm voice.

"I'll put them in interrogation," Barney turned.

"Jesus Christ, they're not being interrogated," Cal started, but Megan put a hand on his arm. He looked from it to her pleading gaze. "Fine, whatever," he grumbled as they followed the sheriff through the door.

"You boys look like crap," Cal offered when they were brought into the small room, furnished with only a table and a few chairs. They were all sunburned, the result of being too manly for the sunscreen Megan had continually offered them yesterday. Harold, with his red hair and fair complexion, was the worse. White skin circled their blood-shot eyes from sunglasses and Cal felt a stab of guilt at not limiting the beer they had consumed.

150

"Man, where have you been?" Tom groused. "We tried to call you first, like you said."

Cal sent him a warning look as Barney walked in with more chairs. At this point he wasn't at all sure the sheriff could be trusted, especially now that he knew the man had run a make on Megan. Even if the sheriff left, Cal knew the room was probably bugged.

"Sorry, kid. Phone died." Cal gestured them to the chairs and pulled one out for Megan. He remained standing. "So your rooms were broken into. Anything taken?"

He knew Harold recognized the indifference in his voice to be anything but. "No, sir. Doesn't appear so. We had our money with us and there wasn't much else of value."

Richard looked like he wanted to say something so Cal jumped in. "Any other rooms get hit?" he asked the sheriff, who had decided to stay in the room.

"Yeah, a few on the same floor." He gave the information reluctantly.

"Then it doesn't appear that these particular boys were targeted," Cal said. "Did you take the others into protective custody, too, or just these three?"

Barney narrowed his gaze at the sarcasm in Cal's voice. "It's these three who are into something." He pointed. "They knew about Dough."

"Sheriff," Cal said with an exaggerated sigh. "They're playing an online computer game and that other kid was involved. That does not make them suspect in every B&E in the county."

"Spring break is long over and I've got no use for college kids causing trouble."

"We're not," Richard started but Cal put a hand on his shoulder.

"I want them out of my town." He huffed.

This is too easy, Cal thought. "You're absolutely right, Sheriff. If you will release them, I'll make sure they get into Boston and on the first flights home."

He saw Megan's eyes widen but she knew enough to keep her mouth shut. The sheriff, not knowing what was going on but suspecting something, narrowed his gaze.

"Why would you do that?"

Cal smiled for the first time since waking up that morning. "I'm going that way. Besides, I'm just helping out a fellow officer of the law."

* * *

"Don't say a word." Megan heard him caution the boys as they collected their belongings from the receptionist. They looked as though he was a parent, reprimanding them for bad behavior, but she thought different. She figured they all realized the break in was more than just random, and he didn't want anything said in front of the sheriff.

Megan stood in awe as Cal efficiently saw to the paperwork and ushered the boys out the front door. When he wasn't angry, he could be terribly official, she thought as he even shook Barney's hand on the front step.

They remained quiet on the short drive to the resort, the deputy's car following close behind.

"Wait here," Cal said to her when he parked. "This shouldn't take long."

The deputy followed them through the entrance and Megan sat, gaze glued to the sliding glass doors. Her phone rang and she almost ignored it but saw it was Jeff.

"Hey, where are you guys? I've been trying to call Cal."

"Sorry, he got a call this morning about a case he's working and we're," should she say where? "We're out of town for the moment. What's up?"

"Ah, the holiday's over, huh? Anyway, Mom and Dad are heading back to Arizona in the morning so I thought we'd take them to the Barking Crab tonight for dinner." The restaurant was down on the waterfront and an outdoor favorite in the summer.

"No tours?" she asked, as Jeff had really cut back over the last three days while his parents visited.

"Oh, hell, yes, but I've got people to cover. I'll post a regular schedule as soon as I can and we'll be back on track."

Megan saw Tom coming out of the resort, carrying a canvas bag and his computer, followed by the others. The deputy brought up the rear. As Cal and the boys walked toward the truck, the deputy sauntered over to his car, leaned against it and crossed his arms over his chest. It seemed as though he wasn't sure they would all leave his town. Either that or he planned to escort them out.

"Gotta go, Jeff. I'll tell Cal."

The minute the guys piled in the back and Cal got behind the steering wheel, she turned to ask, "So what's really going on?"

Cal shook his head. She looked toward the back seat. All three had their mouths pinched tightly shut, looking straight ahead.

"Okay," she dragged the word out as she turned around and buckled her seat belt. "Nice day for a ride, huh?"

Cal stopped at a rest area half way back to Boston. "Out," he said as he turned to the kids. Without a word, they obediently got out with their gear.

"Cal!" Megan gasped, "You can't leave them on the side of the road." She had unbuckled her seatbelt and was grabbing the door handle.

"Whoa." He caught her arm. "They're not going anywhere." He pitched his voice low. "I didn't have time to check their bags at the hotel, so I do it now, before we get back to town."

He could tell she still didn't understand, but accepted his work, quietly getting out of the truck and coming around to where the guys had their bags and computers spread out on a picnic table. While he went through each bag, inspecting each article of clothing and examining every flip flop, Tom, Dick and Harry opened their lap tops and started searching.

One by one, their thumbs came up and they shut down their computers. He had been lucky, too, but in a different way. He silently held up three tracking devices, all small and round, easily mistaken for a button, which is where he had found them, fastened to shirts.

Mouths opened and he quickly put a finger to his lips. "Glad you had a good time out in the harbor yesterday," he said casually.

"Hmm, yeah. Your sailboat is awesome," Tom added.

Cal looped his hand in a *keep going* gesture, and as Megan and the others chatted about the holiday, he went about hiding the tracking devices on unsuspecting tourists' vehicles. Whoever had planted them would be going in three different directions before they realized it was a false trail.

Only when they got back in the truck did he feel they could have an ordinary conversation.

"Sorry about that, Megan," he said as they pulled back out onto the highway. "I didn't think about bugs until I saw the damage to the rooms. Then I had only enough time to warn the guys to keep their mouths shut."

Looking into his rear view mirror, he asked in general, "Did you find anything on your computers?"

Tom answered. "We all have firewalls and passwords, not just for the game but for everything on our hard drives. Our computers had been turned on, but no one breached our operating systems."

"Are you sure?"

"Yeah, man," Richard said. "Tell him we can do that, Megan."

Cal glanced quickly sideways, brow arched. Megan smiled at him. "They can do that, Cal."

"Harrumph." Cal wasn't as computer savvy as he could be, but it just wasn't his thing. That didn't mean he didn't appreciate the fact there were people like Megan who could wrap their brain around that technology.

"You missed the airport turnoff," she said casually, pointing out the window.

He didn't answer as he turned onto Endicott.

"You never intended to put them on a plane, did you?"

He shook his head as he pulled into the parking at his condo. "Not until we know what the hell is going on and who is behind it."

"Welcome to the Garrett Ritz," he said as he ushered them inside. "There are plenty of rooms upstairs for you to store your gear, but you'll have to share the bathroom."

"You have an upstairs?" Megan asked as she followed him into the kitchen. He opened the fridge, then the cupboards.

"We need groceries."

"Cal." She turned him toward her. "Talk to me."

"Yes, there's an upstairs. I lived here with several other guys during college. When the complex went private, I bought this condo. I thought about renting out the other rooms, but decided I liked the privacy."

She was shaking her head. "That's not what I meant. Bringing them here; getting groceries?"

He kissed the tip of her nose. "Here I can keep an eye on them."

He told himself it was police business but he knew by the expression on her face that she was about to say something sappy so tried to head her off. "Want to make a grocery run?"

She gave him a look, then sighed. "I can do that, but then I have to get home. I haven't been online all day, so that's a priority. Oh, and I forgot. We're going to the Barking Crab for dinner with your folks tonight."

"Tonight?" he asked as he tugged her close, bumping his hips against hers.

"Hey, man, this is a really cool place." Richard's voice came from the living room and Cal reluctantly stepped away.

Megan chuckled. "There went your privacy."

* * *

Megan put on a new sundress she had bought last week, enjoying the feel of the silk as it slid down her body.

Although it had a built-in bra, she felt sexy with just the tiny straps crisscrossing her chest to hold up the bodice. The mint green set off her suntan, and the knee length showed off her long legs. She pinned her hair back with combs, sprayed on a light fragrance, and slipped into her sandals. She hoped Cal appreciated her efforts, as he usually saw her in shorts or her colonial costume, although he did say there was something about that costume. She grinned at her reflection in the mirror.

"Ready?" Stacy came out of the bathroom as she was sharing Megan's room while her parents were here.

"The question is whether the Barking Crab is ready for us." Megan looped her arm in Stacy's as they went to join the others.

"Don't you two look lovely," Sharon said when they came into the kitchen. "Isn't it nice to dress up once in a while? Today, everything is just so casual." She shook her head.

"Well, I'm all for the short shorts and bikini tops," Jeff grinned, only to have his dad bop him on the head.

"Yeah, if you only looked good in them," Cal quipped and they all laughed as they spilled out the door.

Cal grabbed Megan's hand and held her back from the others. "You look more beautiful than all the flowers in the garden."

Megan's heart caught in her throat. "That is so sweet."

He frowned. "I can be sweet."

She leaned in and kissed him; a gentle rub of the lips that held a promise of more. "Then where are your roommates?"

"I left them home." He dropped his arm around her shoulders. "I'm not that sweet."

Chapter 16

Megan had sold an article to *Boston Now* magazine about Jeff's tour company, emphasizing the river tour. It wasn't her usual type of article, as there was no undercover work involved, but Jeff was excited and Megan was happy to deposit a check in the bank. If she had realized just how much it would increase his tour requests, she might have held off submitting it. She had already been doing more tours, and now he had hired a few other people to handle the overflow.

"You are the best!" He hugged her. "And you're on again tonight," he said on his way out the door.

"Again?" She had been working almost every night, either down town or to the river. Since Cal worked days, they hardly ever saw each other. Even when he came to the Pub at the end of her tours, he was tired, she was tired, and there were three impressionable young men staying at his condo so she was staying at the B&B. They didn't have a chance.

"Still playing that game?" Matt asked as he walked right in the minute Jeff left. Helping himself to a beer from the fridge, he wandered over and tried to peer at her computer screen. She lowered it until it almost closed.

"Stacy's not here," she said. Matt had been spending an inordinate amount of time here, and although he had never made any more suggestive remarks, something about him put Megan's hackles up.

He shrugged off her comment. "Just talked to her on the phone. She's on the way home."

He sat down across from her.

"Finding any treasure?"

She narrowed her gaze. She was sure she hadn't said anything about the game, or treasure, and although she had cautioned Stacy not to mention the game, she couldn't know what her friend might say to a boyfriend.

"How do you know about any game?"

One shoulder lifted then dropped. "Friend of a friend. I'm into that technology, you know."

She hadn't known. He had never said what he did for a living and frankly, she hadn't cared enough to ask. She did now. "Into technology; how exactly?"

"Computer software design," he said smugly.

"Really?" For just a minute, she thought about getting his advice on how to locate the creator of this particular game.

"Blogs, website templates; that sort of thing."

"Oh." A far cry from designing an interactive game, she thought. She rubbed her hands on her shorts. Her fingers itched to get back on line as she was really close to finding the *DragonFyre's* fortress, but she didn't dare open her computer with him sitting directly across from her, eyeing her like he knew something she didn't.

"Matt?" Stacy walked in, hidden behind a huge box of groceries. Matt jumped up to take it and set it on the counter.

"I saw your car outside. What are you doing here in the middle of the day, in the middle of the week?"

"Just checking in, sweetheart." He dropped a kiss on her forehead.

Something in his voice, in his demeanor, made Megan want to gag. She stuffed the laptop into her carrying case and stood. "I'm going for a walk," she said to Stacy.

"Aren't you on tour again tonight?" Stacy asked. "I'd think you'd get enough exercise walking to the river and back."

"I need the fresh air." She smiled sweetly and ducked out the back door.

Five minutes later she was down at the subway, waiting for the red line. Not exactly fresh air, she thought as some unidentifiable odor hit her nostrils. She hopped aboard the minute the doors opened, getting off several stops later.

She pulled the key out of the door as she pushed it open. When she had tried to give Cal his keys back that day in the rain, he had told her to keep them, just in case. Today was that time, and although she knew the guys were there, she didn't know if they would have opened the door.

"Hey, Megan." Three voices reached her the minute the door closed.

"How did you know it wasn't Cal?" she asked, coming around the corner to where they sat at the dining room table.

"Cal showed us how he has it rigged so there's a mirror in every room that shows the front door, or shows the reflection of it from another mirror," Tom said, pointing to a mirror on the wall. "Really cool detective stuff, huh?"

"I'm thinking of a way to add them to my fortress," Richard said. "That way I can see someone coming."

"You can see because it's a computer screen, idiot." Harold said good-naturedly.

Megan ignored their bantering as she wandered into the kitchen, then out through the dining room to the living room. Those mirrors hadn't been in place the last time she had been here. She was sure of that. It was just another way he was protecting those boys.

"Anything new and exciting?" she asked in general when she came back to the table.

"Not much. We can't seem to make progress on the *Rattler*," Tom said. "We're sure he's in Texas, but every lead is wrong and his fortress keeps getting higher."

"Nobody's missing today, anyway. Where's Cal?"

"Try Oklahoma," Megan said.

All three looked up from their computer screens. "Why is Cal in Oklahoma?" Harold asked.

"What?" Megan shook her head. "He didn't say. Oh, no. I meant to look for the *Rattler* in Oklahoma. I think they have rattlesnake roundups there."

"How do you *know* all this stuff?" Tom said in awe.

"When you get old, your brain is full of useless trivia."

"You're not *that* old," he replied. "Are you?"

Megan was saved from answering when her phone rang. "Hey," she answered.

"Are you at the house?" Cal asked.

"No. Actually I'm at your place. What's up?"

"Absolutely nothing. We thought we had a lead on our missing person in Las Vegas, but it turns out she's an eighty-two year old grandma. The police located her today on the strip, tucking dollar bills into the G-strings of male strippers."

Megan started laughing. "Eighty-two? Didn't your techs filter for age?"

She could hear Cal chuckle. "They did, although we're only assuming the game is limited by age in that younger people are into that technology. However, in this case, the original report had transposed the numbers in her age."

"I want to be her when I get that old," Megan mused.

"Like hell," Cal hissed. "You want a G-string, I'll give you one."

"You have one?" She giggled, thoroughly enjoying the sexy banter as she hadn't seen Cal in days and missed him terribly. Remembering the boys, she walked into the kitchen and turned her back. "Would you dance for me, too?"

She heard him groan. "Meg, you're killing me here. And I just called to tell you I'd be working late." She heard him sigh mightily on the other end of the line.

It echoed her own. "It doesn't matter. Ever since my article came out, Jeff has been inundated, so I'm on again tonight."

"That's what you get for trying to make a living," he tossed her own thoughts back at her. "I'll try to make it to the Pub, but we're waiting to hear from L. A. and they're three hours earlier time-wise, not that anyone around here actually works only nine to five."

"Is it all right if I see if the guys want to go on the tour with me?"

"Who; Tom, Dick and Harry? Are you trying to step out on me, woman?"

160

"Oh, please. They've got nothing on you," she said, paused, then added, "well, maybe a few years." She ended on a laugh.

"You are so going to get it." His threat, low and sexy, sent shivers up Megan's spine.

"Promises, promises."

"You'd better believe it," he replied. There was a short silence and Megan thought the call had dropped, but then he was back. "Look, I've got to go. Just be careful. There shouldn't be a problem as long as you're with a crowd."

"I will. See you later, maybe."

"I can always hope." He hung up.

Megan wandered back into the dining room to find all heads bent over their computers.

"Do you want to do a tour with me tonight?" she asked the group in general. Only Harold's head popped up.

"What tour?" he asked.

"It's about a family from Boston's history. We go down to the river." She realized she really did want their company, so she added, "We might even see a ghost."

Now Tom and Richard looked at her. "Right. Like there are no such things," Tom said.

"You never know," she smiled.

"Megan, they are figments of people's imaginations," Richard added.

He sounded just like Cal.

"And the game you're playing isn't?" Crap. Now *she* sounded just like Cal.

"We can see and interact with what's on the screen, even though we know it's not real."

"Okay, fine, but I've got to go. Lock up after me and don't forget to eat." She turned to leave.

"Wait. I'll go with you," Harold said, quickly shutting down his computer. "I need a break."

* * *

Megan left Harold with Stacy in the kitchen while she went to change. She remembered to call Dr. Farrington while on the subway and he said he would be happy to accompany them on the tour. By the time she was ready, several tourists were gathered in the sitting room, him among them. She introduced him to Harold, mentioning Harvard, but refrained from saying anything about the man's avocation. They appeared to hit it off instantly.

Only a sliver of moon peeked in and out of the clouds as she led the group down a side street toward the river. It would be a new moon in a few days, and while Jeff loved the night tours then, they always caused Megan to feel uneasy. There weren't many street lights along the way, and the river area was always dark, which was all the more reason for the candle lanterns they carried. It wasn't always about ambience, she thought wryly.

"But tonight, there was a traitor among them," she said just before she covered her lantern and the re-enactors began their play. When Toni screamed, the words, not the fake scream, sent a chill down her back. She looked quickly over the group as she recalled Laurie saying almost the same words to her. She couldn't make out the faces in the dark, but hadn't recalled anything peculiar when greeting the guests back at the house. That didn't make her less anxious to get done.

As quickly as she could, she finished her dialogue and pointed the crowd down the path to the pub. She let Gary, the other guide, take point and she brought up the rear, walking next to Dr. Farrington; Harold on her other side. She started to ask them what they thought of the tour when someone grabbed her arm and swung her around.

"Hey!" Thinking it was Cal sneaking up on her, she smiled in greeting.

It wasn't Cal. Tall, with dark hair and eyes, the man stood menacingly over her. "Where is the treasure?" he asked in a heavily accented voice.

"Let go of me," she said, swinging out her foot to kick him. Unfortunately her long skirts prevented it from being effective.

"Tell me." He shook her.

"Hey, there." Dr. Farrington stepped forward. "Let go of the lady."

The man reached out his other hand and flattened it on the professor's chest, shoving him backward into Harold and they both fell to the ground.

Why is no one coming to help, Megan thought frantically. She turned to yell at the group but the man clamped a hand over her mouth. At that moment, the little black box that the professor had hanging around his neck started beeping and little lights began blinking rapidly. In the next instant, she and her attacker were enveloped in a swirling green haze. Caught by surprise, he released her and she stumbled back, but the green haze remained on him, spinning around him like a dust devil while he swatted at his head and ears and yelled in some foreign language.

Megan couldn't have moved if her life depended on it. She felt an arm go around her and glanced at Harold, who stood by her side, eyes the size of saucers. She thought she might have even smiled as the green haze slowly dissipated, leaving the man stumbling in a circle, still tugging at his ears and mumbling. When he realized nothing was there, he stared at her, said something she thought was probably vile, and turned to flee down the darkened path.

"Are you all right?" Dr. Farrington came up to her, the box quiet once again.

Harold spoke before she could form words. "I thought you were fucking, whoops, sorry, but you were kidding me. That was her, wasn't it? Man, that was crazier than a computer game. Wait till the guys hear what they missed."

"She was here?" the professor asked, his voice quieter than Harold's, but just as excited.

"Oh, yeah," Megan replied turning to the professor with a huge grin. "With vengeance! Did you see her?"

He shook his head and she could see the disappointment on his face. "I always thought if I should encounter a ghost, I would be able to see it, but that was not the case." He held up the little black box. "I did, however, get recordings of the electromagnetic energy she emitted and shall have that to study." He looked owl eyed over the top of his glasses at Harold. "Did you actually see her?"

"No, but something was making that man wiggle and yell and spin in circles." He paused before adding, "You're not supposed to *see* ghosts anyway. That doesn't mean they're not there."

Megan laughed as she looped her arm with the professor's. "Let's talk over a beer at the pub."

"I could use one," Harold said, still shaking his head in astonishment.

"I will be most happy to buy," the professor quipped.

* * *

Cal watched the tour group enter the pub. Why was she always at the end? He scanned the crowd, not finding Harold either. When he'd gotten back to the condo, Tom had told him Harold was with Megan. So where were they? And why was his head telling him everything was fine and his gut was telling him different?

She came in, turning to talk to someone behind her. Her face was glowing with excitement and he thought it must have been a good tour, until he saw Keith come in next, followed by Harold. He might have guessed what was up, but the way Harold was talking and gesturing, twitching almost like a rabid dog, left no doubt in his mind.

Great. All he needed was a lonely ghost making an appearance. Now when he pulled Megan off the tour schedule, he'd have not only Jeff on his case but the professor as well. He got up from the bar and moved toward them. It couldn't be helped. He would do anything to insure Megan's safety, even if it meant confronting a two hundred year old ghost.

Chapter 17

"Ah, Detective Garrett," the professor began as Cal stopped at the table they had chosen. But Harold practically burst into song.

"You should have seen it, Detective It was so totally awesome! Megan's ghost swirled around her and this guy who grabbed her—"

"Grabbed her?" Cal asked, his voice a low menace. He looked at Megan, then the Professor. "What's he talking about? Who grabbed you? What the hell is going on?" His reason for getting to the pub for Harold and Megan was immediately forgotten. Screw the game; this was a real threat.

"Megan?" He raised a brow in question.

"Harold, why don't you and the Professor go get some drinks?" she asked instead of answering hm. "There'll be time for rehashing your experience in just a bit."

When the other two left the table, Cal searched Megan's face. Her cheeks still held a faint color, her eyes were sparkling, but he noticed that her hands shook slightly until she clasped them together on the table.

"Laurie was there again tonight," she began.

"To hell with some ghost," Cal hissed. "Who grabbed you?"

She ducked her head at his rebuke, so he reached out and put his hand over hers. They were icy cold. "I'm sorry I yelled but I need to know what's going on."

She looked at him. "That's just it. The two things are related...somehow. We were bringing up the tail end of the tour and some guy out of nowhere grabbed me. In the next instance, we were enveloped with this green haze and the man started swatting his head and ears as though a thousand bees were swarming him."

"Are you hurt?" His gaze roved over her.

She shook her head. "That's what's so strange. It only seemed to affect him. He let go of me, stumbled to his knees, then when the haze disappeared, he got up and ran off, yelling in some foreign language."

"It was a South American dialect," Harold said as he and the Professor returned with the drinks, setting them on the table. Harold took a swallow of the stout ale before he continued. "I think maybe Brazil."

"How the hell do you know that?" Cal sucked down half his beer, trying to get a handle on the emotions swirling in his gut.

"I studied linguistics," Harold answered matter of fact. "The majority of languages in South America were originally derived from the Spanish or Portuguese but through time different dialects of the colonial language developed in individual countries."

"You have quite an ear, young man," Professor Farrington commented. "I didn't understand anything he said other than something about a treasure. But the tone of his voice was rude and very threatening."

"Cal." Megan was now frowning. She slowly rotated the glass of beer between her hands but didn't drink. "I didn't understand anything the man said, either, but I keep hearing the same accent over and over." She sat pondering, then her expression cleared. "Here at the pub – the night that man's beer spilled – he had the same accent. And the man who came to the house wanting a room. But each time it was a different man."

Cal took a deep breath, looking from Harold to the Professor to Megan. "Do you think you could describe the one tonight to a police artist?" Everyone nodded. He looked at Megan. "You're the only one, of you three, who saw the other men. It'll be up to you to give us something to go on; something I can send out and post at the precinct." He paused, remembering his initial reason for coming to get Megan.

"Okay. That's one problem we have to work with but I actually came because we may have a break in the case. There's a missing girl reported in L. A. who seems to fit the profile we set up. A detective there is going to interview her family to see if she was into online games; where she might have gone; any known associates. That sort of thing."

"Do you have a name?" Harold asked, his face troubled. "Regardless of the fact we play online, there are some groups we all belong to and we have gaming sessions once in a while at some local place."

Both Cal's brows rose. "We're talking Los Angeles, Harold, not Porchello, whose residents could all board the Titanic with room to spare." When he saw the kid's expression, he dropped his head in defeat. How the hell did he get tangled up in this mess? He felt Megan's hand on his leg and knew.

"Lauren Harding," Cal said, and watched as Harold seemed to dissolve into the chair. He swayed, his face turned white, which made his freckles stand out all the more, and for a minute Cal thought he was going to throw up.

"Easy, kid." He put a hand on his shoulder to steady him. "Put your head down."

"It can't be," he heard Harold mumble. "Oh, god."

Cal looked over at the Professor, momentarily changing the subject to give Harold a chance to recover. "Did you see your ghost tonight, Keith?"

The man shook his head. "As I told Megan, I had always hoped I would have the opportunity, but apparently, at least with this particular spirit, females are more susceptible. I'm not at all sure that man even knew what was attacking him." He tapped the black box on the table. "But I did get recordings of some sort, and will enjoy seeing what they can tell us."

Cal rubbed his temples where a headache was forming. He couldn't recall previous cases giving him headaches, but knew exactly why this one was different. One reason sat on his left, slowly raising his head and taking a sip of the water a waitress had brought. The other reason, indeed the absolute foremost reason, sat on his right holding his heart in her hands.

"We need sketches of Megan's attacker. That's a priority, but I also want to find out who killed John Dough, and that means dealing with whoever is causing havoc with this game." He turned to Harold. "Are you ready to talk?"

He nodded. "I should have connected it – Lauren Harding and *Comedian2*."

"What do you mean?"

"Lauren Harding – Laurel and Hardy – two comedians?"

"Oh, no," Megan said.

Cal could think of more explicit words. He felt like Jim Carey in *The Truman Show*.

"So you know her?"

He nodded again. "But she didn't use that avatar on the games we've played. That's why it didn't connect. Besides, *Comedian2* is using the Bahia Emerald, and I can't see that Lauren would have anything to do with that, so that part really doesn't make sense."

Cal stood. "Okay. The first order of business is getting a sketch of the man from tonight while the details are still fresh in your minds. Professor, if you wouldn't mind, can you come to headquarters with us now?"

The man nodded.

"While we're there, Harold, I want you to talk to a detective, and give him everything you can think of on Lauren Harding. Since we know she's a player, he'll want all your online contacts; their names and emails; phone numbers if you have them. He'll see that it gets forwarded to the L. A. police. We need to find her before something happens," he said, refusing to say out loud – *before she ends up like John Dough.*

* * *

Why do I need sleep? Megan stole a glance at the clock on the wall. *It's only three in the morning.* She

168

looked longingly at the sofa set against the wall in the conference room where Cal had put her when they got to the precinct. The upholstery was stained and it looked really lumpy. She tilted sideways. Maybe just a little catnap...

"How would you describe the man at the house?" asked Fletcher, the police artist. He sat, hands poised over the I-pad, entirely too perky for this hour of the night.

"I thought we were talking about the man from tonight?"

"Done. Between the Professor and Harold, I think we have him nailed."

"Alfred Hitchcock." Her eyes drifted closed. Where was Cal? She really needed to get home and go to bed. She had texted Stacy from the Pub, but only told her that she was with Cal, not where they were going or why.

"Miss Anderson?" A hand touched her shoulder.

"Hmm?" She crossed her arms on the table and laid her head down. The adrenalin rush she had had when Laurie appeared to save her from that thug had long since vanished, leaving her totally drained.

"Up you go."

She squawked as she was grabbed from behind and pulled right out of the chair. Reflexively she swung her elbow back, connecting with a very hard jaw. Her eyes popped open.

"Feel better?" Cal grinned at her, his arms totally supporting her as her legs felt like rubber.

"When you let go of me, I'm going to kill you." Her heart was still pounding.

"Well, then, it looks like I'll just have to hold you until Fletcher is done." The grin remained, and although she protested, he sat in the chair and plopped her right down on his lap.

She glanced at the sketch artist when he discretely coughed. A rather comical expression crossed his face at Cal's possessive manhandling. Even if her brain was in a fog, she knew there would be office betting pools going by morning.

Yawning, she laid her head on his shoulder. "You're much more comfortable than the chair."

"You know, if you fall asleep this will just take longer."

He shook her gently. "Megan, come on. I've already sent the Professor home, and Harold is in my office, crashed on the couch."

She sat up and glared at him. "You let them sleep?"

He was rubbing her back and it felt incredibly good. She shrugged her shoulders and arched.

"You saw all three men. The others only saw tonight's guy."

Megan knew she would never get any sleep until she gave him what he wanted.

"Fine. The man at the house looked like Alfred Hitchcock, like I originally told you. Bald, beady eyes, rotund. Eyes were dark, maybe brown. He was about Stacy's height."

"Five two," Cal said to Fletcher.

"The man at the pub was tall and thin. Well, he was sitting, but you could tell, you know, that he was tall." She was rambling. She gave herself a mental shake, momentarily clearing the cobwebs. "He had dark hair with a receding hairline and a moustache. Oh, and his eyebrows were arched, not straight across. He reminded me of someone, but I can't exactly remember when I'm brain dead." She elbowed Cal in the stomach for emphasis. She saw Fletcher try to hide a smile.

"She's not much good when she gets cranky like this," Cal said to Fletcher, his humor coming out in his voice.

Megan glared at him.

"Use what you have and start running all three through the system. With similar accents, they have to be associated." He stood, setting Megan on her feet but keeping his arm around her waist. "Let's get you and the kid home. Thanks, Fletch."

Megan walked like a zombie down the hall to Cal's office. He didn't let go of her as he whistled for Harold, who popped up like a jack-in-the-box.

170

"Are you finally done?" he asked. "Geez, Megan, you look like—"

"Don't say it," she interrupted. "In fact, don't even think it."

The minute Cal closed the door when she got into the truck, she leaned her head on the window and shut her eyes.

"Hey." He poked her arm when he got in. "It's five minutes to the condo. Don't go to sleep now."

"Go...away." She emphasized each word with a swat of her hand.

"Tell me about the ghost tonight."

Megan sighed. He just wasn't going to leave her alone. She rolled her head, trying to get the kinks out of her neck and he reached over and began massaging it for her.

"That will not redeem you, you know."

She could see his grin flash in the dark. "It's all I've got for now, baby. Seriously, I want to know about the ghost."

"It wasn't a person tonight. It was the green haze I've seen before, only this time she didn't just float around. She swirled. If I hadn't known what it was, I would have been on the ground right along with that man."

"It was like they were in the middle of an invisible tornado," Harold piped up from the back seat. "Scary and awesome at the same time."

Megan had thought quite a bit about Laurie's presence at the river and the other times she had made herself known to Megan.

"I don't know why Laurie has attached herself to me. When we were young, Stacy and I always just thought she was imaginary."

"Does Stacy see her?" Cal glanced quickly her way then his gaze went back to the road as they turned the corner to his condo.

"No, but she does believe me." She saw Cal frown and regretted her words. She wouldn't have said that if she weren't so tired. "Sorry. Anyway, every time Laurie has appeared, it's been to warn me, although I have no idea why. Then tonight, she became a dervish and saved me from that thug. It's like she's become my guardian angel or something."

She squinted when Cal opened his door and the interior lights came on. "Cal, I just want to go home. This is your place."

He didn't answer until he had come around the truck and opened her door. "It's late; too much happened tonight I can't explain, and I just don't want you out of my sight. Okay?"

She wasn't about to argue. Harold was already bouncing by the time they got to the door.

"Just wait till the guys hear this! I couldn't begin to explain in a text, so I just told them I'd talk to them when I got back."

Cal opened the door and turned on a light, fully expecting the other two to be in bed. Instead, two heads popped up from the sofa where they had apparently tried to wait up.

"What time is it?" Richard asked.

"After four," Cal answered and Megan groaned. She hadn't pulled an all nighter since college.

"What happened?" Tom asked, eyes wide.

"Wait till you hear," Harold started.

"Take it upstairs, guys" Cal said. "Just keep it quiet so the old folks can get some sleep."

Megan watched as all three headed down the hall for the stairs. Cal turned her around and pulled her close, his hands sliding up and down her back. As good as it felt, she couldn't muster enough energy to tilt her head for a kiss, so she contented herself with laying her head on his shoulder and absorbing his caresses.

"Let's get you to bed," he said, leading her down the hall to his bedroom.

"Cal, I can't stay here with you," she finally managed to get out. "Not with the boys right upstairs."

"Sh, it's okay." He kissed her temple. "I'll sleep on the couch."

"That helps in your redemption," she murmured as he unbuttoned and slid her skirt and petticoats to the floor.

"Arms up," was all he said as he tugged her bodice over her head, leaving her in camisole and panties. "Get in." He held up the sheet and she crawled into bed.

"Oh, god. That feels so good." She closed her eyes with a sigh.

She felt the bed give as he sat down beside her, bracing one arm on the opposite side as he leaned in close.

"You scared five years off my life tonight," he murmured as he kissed her brow.

"Only five?" she smiled, not opening her eyes.

"You're right. My entire life would be over if anything had happened to you."

She did open her eyes then. His brow was furrowed in worry. His fingers slid over her forehead and down her cheek, tucking her hair behind her ear. His gaze caressed her as though memorizing her features.

She reached up to cup his cheek with her palm. She didn't know if it would help or cause him to become even more possessive, but she gave him the only reassurance she could.

"I love you Cal Garrett, and I know you'll take care of me."

Chapter 18

Cal's internal clock woke him right at seven, as it always did, even on weekends. He sat on the edge of the couch rubbing his face, wondering how in hell he'd get through the day on less than three hours sleep. He stood, raising his arms above his head then bending forward to touch the floor, stretching his muscles and hearing his back pop. Hell, he was getting old. It wasn't that long ago that he could be up days at a time if he was working a case. And his body didn't creak.

He started the coffee, then walked down the hall to his room. Quietly opening the door, he gazed across the room to where Megan lay, curled on her side, exactly where he usually slept. Her hair spilled across his pillow and he longed to bury his face in its silky length.

One long, sexy leg poked out from beneath the sheet. His groan made her stir but she didn't awaken. She said she loved him, he thought as he soundlessly walked to his dresser for clean clothes. Had she meant it, or had it been a reaction to the events of the night?

He turned the shower to scalding and groaned again as he stood under the jets, letting the water pound his tired muscles and free the cobwebs from his brain. It might be better if they weren't involved, because his growing fear for her was a detriment to clear thinking on the case. If his Captain found out...hell, there was no way the man wouldn't know because little got past Fletcher and Cal had seen the man's expression as he held Megan on his lap.

It didn't matter, he realized as he toweled off. No way was he going to stay away from Megan, and he would certainly not stop investigating John Dough's murder. Both were now tied to the game and he wouldn't rest until he knew Megan was safe.

Pulling on jeans and a tee shirt, he ran a quick comb through his hair and padded barefoot back through the bedroom. He didn't look at the bed. It would be far too easy to lie down and curl up against her, losing himself in her softness.

In the kitchen, he poured a cup of coffee, listening to the quiet surrounding him. No one had surfaced from upstairs either and he figured those three probably hadn't gotten any sleep. They would have rehashed Harold's experience with the ghost, and then most likely tried to figure out why Lauren Harding was missing. He had gotten used to having them around, he thought surprisingly, as he had always coveted his privacy. They were good kids, reminding him of Jeff and himself at their ages. Then, they had had dreams of saving the world; him through police work and Jeff through preserving history.

He had just started mixing up pancake batter when a sound caused him to still. He glanced toward the hall but no one appeared. He cocked his head to the side as another *click* came from the front room.

Two steps to the left and he had his back pressed against the pantry door. Someone was trying to get in. He silently released the safety on his gun as his gaze steadied on the mirror hanging on the far end of the dining room, reflecting the front door. He could see the door crack open, a muscular arm and shoulder appearing. He waited another second, wanting the perpetrator fully inside, not fleeing back down the hall.

He took a breath; held it, then slowly let it out.

"Stop right there!" He stepped around the corner, arms straight and gun steady.

"What the fuck?" Jeff squawked, dropping his keys on the floor.

Cal jerked his arms upward, pointing his gun at the ceiling, automatically slipping the safety on. "God damn it, Jeff, I could have shot you!"

"I would have knocked if I had thought you were up," he groused, bending down to get his keys. "Since when do you walk around your own place fully armed?"

Cal's heart was only then beginning to slow. He sucked in his breath as he slid his gun back into its holster at the small of his back. "Since someone attacked Megan last night, on *your* tour." Needing an outlet for the frustration and anger he felt, he lit into his brother. "She's got no business wandering around town in the dark. *You've* got no business putting people in jeopardy with your damn tours."

"What?"

Cal could hear the surprise in his brother's voice.

"I don't...there's never been any trouble." Jeff's voice shook. "Shit, Cal, you know I would never put the girls in danger. I don't even know what happened."

Cal could see the crestfallen look on his brother's face. He rolled his shoulders to release the tension. "Okay, fine. What the hell are you doing here anyway?"

Jeff had wandered into the kitchen behind Cal and was helping himself to a cup of coffee. "Stacy said Megan hadn't come home after the tour last night so I figured she was here. I need her to," he paused, glancing anywhere but at Cal.

"To what?"

"Uh."

Cal looked up from the griddle where he had just poured pancake batter. He knew that guilty expression. "No. Hell, no. She's not doing any more tours."

"This is day time."

Cal was shaking his head. "It doesn't matter. Someone attacked her last night, and prior to that some guy grabbed her at the pub. Someone is targeting her on your tours, asking about treasure..."

He jerked the griddle off the burner and practically threw it onto the back of the stove.

"Son of a bitch, that's it."

"What's it?" Jeff asked just as Cal's cell rang.

"Hello," he growled.

"Garrett, I want you down here right away." His boss's voice was urgent. "And bring Megan Anderson and that kid with you."

"Boss, nobody got any sleep last night. You probably read the reports, so you know—"

"Are they at your place?"

Cal hesitated. "Yeah."

"Okay. I'll send a patrol car over so someone's there with them. But I need you here, ten minutes ago."

"Why the hell do they need police protection?" Cal asked but the phone clicked. He stared at it for a minute wondering what the hell was going on.

"What?"

He left Jeff's question hanging as he hurried down the hall and into his room for a shirt. He thought about waking Megan to tell her what he had just pieced together, but decided if he did, she would want to go with him. Until he knew why McGuire wanted him down at headquarters so urgently, and why the police protection, she would be better off here.

He came back out, buttoning his shirt. "Jeff, I need you to stay here until a patrolman comes. Something's up at the precinct but more importantly, I think I know why Megan is being targeted."

"What's going on?" Jeff's voice was quiet.

"In your script, you reference things and people disappearing after Laurie was taken, right? Things, like treasure."

"We never really say there's treasure involved," Jeff said, "although I think people infer that."

Cal waved away his explanation. "I thought I was dealing with two different cases – John Dough's death which is directly tied to the online game the guys are playing, and someone going after Megan because she does tours and they think there is treasure buried around here since 1776." He headed for the door. "But it's all the same. The men going after Megan keep asking about treasure, but it's the treasure in the game, not in Boston."

"I still don't get it," Jeff said.

177

"Someone thinks all the treasures in the game are real and actually held by the players. Someone killed Dough for his treasure; someone is missing because of a treasure, and now Megan and those boys are being pursued because they're in the game."

He turned, hand on the door. "Lock up after me, Jeff. Don't let anyone in and do not let Megan or the others out of your sight." He waited until Jeff looked him squarely in the eyes and nodded.

* * *

"Jeff, what are you doing here?" Megan asked when she got into the kitchen. She looked down; glad she had dug through Cal's drawers for a pair of athletic shorts and a tee instead of coming out in her camisole.

"Breakfast?" Jeff asked, holding up a plate piled high with fragrant, fluffy pancakes. The sound of his voice made her looked more closely at his face.

"Where's Cal?"

"Uh, gone." She watched as he busied himself with turning off the stove and putting the griddle in the sink, all the while not looking at her.

"Where is Cal?" she asked again.

Saved by the bell, she thought, when someone rang at the door. She turned to go answer it but Jeff hurried around her. "Stay here," he said.

She watched as he peered through the peephole before turning the lock and opening the door a mere fraction. He mumbled something and whoever was on the other side replied. Jeff then closed and locked the door again.

Fists on hips, she blocked his way when he turned around. "Jeffery Garrett, what is going on? Who was at the door?"

"I smell pancakes," Tom said and Megan turned to see three rather sleepy boys, hair sticking straight out. Their clothes were wrinkled and as they walked past her, Megan could see that the shirt Harold wore was the same as last night.

"Let's eat," Jeff said, far too cheerfully, digging in the drawer for silverware.

Megan grabbed the plate of pancakes off the counter. "Nobody eats until I know what's going on." She scowled at Jeff.

"What?" Richard said, followed closely by Tom's, "I'm starving."

Harold seemed the only one with a clear head. "Megan, where's Cal?"

"That's what I want to know." She glared at Jeff.

"Eat," he said. "I don't cook that often so you might as well enjoy it while it's hot." He put up a hand when Megan started to protest. "I'll tell you what I know while you eat."

Harold grabbed the pancakes out of her hands as Tom found glasses and Richard the carton of milk from the fridge. They didn't appear near as concerned as she was as they settled down to breakfast.

"Why didn't he wake me if he was going out?" she asked Jeff.

"I don't know that, but since you're not going to quit badgering me, here's what I do know," Jeff said around a mouthful of pancake. "He got a call and something's up at the precinct. He told his boss he wouldn't wake you guys to bring you with him so now there's a patrol car parked outside."

"We're in protective custody, because of that man last night?" Harold asked.

"This is way more exciting than the game," Richard said.

"It's not a game," Jeff replied. "Cal said the man last night and the gaming kid's death are all tied together somehow so you all have to stay here where I can keep an eye on you." He shrugged. "Me and the police outside anyway."

Megan didn't say a word as she mulled over what Jeff had told them. It suddenly made sense. Two of the men with accents had asked her about treasure. She now realized they weren't talking about some long ago crates of guns or other items that Logan Mallory might have stolen from the

British according to the legend they told on the tour. They were after the treasures in the game.

"But the game is fantasy. None of the players actually *have* any treasure. They just have to pick something that's an obscure artifact from the area where they live. Something their local history has documented, but never recovered."

Jeff shrugged. "All I know is Cal said it was the same, so it must be. He's never wrong."

* * *

Cal had been totally off base on what had turned out to be one case, not two, and he couldn't wait to get his team pointed in the right direction. The precinct hummed with activity as he got off the elevator and headed for his boss's office.

Suits. He slowed as McGuire's glass enclosed office came into view. Cal could see him behind his massive desk as three others, all male, all wearing suits, stood in front of him, gesturing. He saw him nod at something one of them said.

What the hell was the FBI doing here, Cal wondered as he kept walking. His gaze locked on his boss's face, hoping for some miraculous insight before he had to knock on the door. It didn't happen.

McGuire waved him in the moment he saw him.

"This is Cal Garrett, the detective on the case." He stood as he spoke, giving Cal the impression he was trying to even the odds. But why? "Detective, these are Agents Norris, Gardner and Morrison."

Cal nodded, then leaned against a short credenza and crossed his legs at the ankles.

"How do you know about Ferreira?" asked one, a rather short guy with graying hair.

"Who?" The name wasn't familiar.

"Look, this is an FBI matter. In fact, it is national security and need-to-know only, so just tell us what you know." The threat came from the tallest of the three, a guy with a buzz cut and military bearing.

There was a reason local authorities didn't like working with the Feds. Cal casually crossed his arms over his chest.

"Let me guess. You're here about the ghost. I didn't know the FBI investigated things like that."

"There's always a wise-ass," said the third guy, who was medium build, just between gray-hair and buzz cut.

"I'm smart enough to know we must have something you want. So as far as need-to-know, you need to tell me what's going on."

"Cal," his boss warned.

Cal put up a hand. "At the moment I have a young woman and three scared young men I'm trying to protect. If you want something from me, I need to know what we're up against. And that they will continue to be protected from whatever the threat is that brought you all down here."

The three looked at each other and seemed to come to some kind of unspoken agreement. "You're just like your old man, Garrett," said gray-hair.

Only a handful of people knew Cal's dad had worked for the FBI years ago. It was a closely guarded family secret because he had exposed countless crime rings and sent plenty of men to prison during his years undercover. Mentioning his dad was like a password to Cal. He unfolded his arms and braced his hands on the desk behind him.

"Who's Ferreira?" he asked.

"You sent a sketch out of him, Silva and Oliveira less than five hours ago."

Cal straightened. "We got a hit on one of Fletcher's sketches?" he asked his boss.

"All three, actually," said buzz cut. Cal needed to put names to these faces.

"Now we're talking," Cal said. "Let's go to my office where I have a scenario board and a coffee pot. I have a feeling we're going to need it."

Fletcher had already tacked up the sketches and accompanying police photos of the three men that Megan, the Professor and Harold had described. Below each were their names and criminal records.

"Hell, they all look like the villains in those old black and white movies I used to watch as a kid," said McGuire as he studied the pictures.

"Well, Megan could only describe one as Alfred Hitchcock." Cal looked at the photos more closely. "I'll be damned. He does look like Hitchcock. And there's Vincent Price and Boris Karloff." He pointed to the other two.

"You're joking, right?" asked Agent Norris. Cal had finally gotten their names straight on the way to his office.

He shook his head. "If you only knew. I've been living inside a television set for months now. You know, sort of like *The Truman Show*?"

Three heads shook in unison, three sets of eyebrows rose in question as though choreographed.

"Just waiting for the three stooges to show up," Cal muttered as he turned back to the board and began writing.

"These three are looking for treasure," he said, bracketing the three pictures with a felt marker. Below them, he wrote *Megan Anderson, Harold Breeze, Thomas Rock, Richard Bier, John Dough and Lauren Harding* in a different color, drawing a box around all the names. "These six, and we don't know how many more, are playing an online computer simulation game that involves fake treasure."

"So you think Ferreira, Silva and Oliveira, one of whom we know attacked Miss Anderson, are trying to get into this game and find real treasure where there is none?"

"They're after the *players* in the game," Cal said, "thinking the players will lead them to a treasure." He starred John Dough's name. "Now this player is dead, Megan is being threatened, and this player," he starred Lauren's name, "is currently a missing person who had claimed online that her treasure is the Bahia Emerald." He was watching the agents closely when he said this and noted recognition in their expressions.

Although he had formed his own hypothesis, he wanted it confirmed. "So now tell me exactly who these assholes are and why you're really here."

Chapter 19

"Well, damn," Megan said, staring at her computer screen. With nothing else to occupy their time, she and the boys had settled down at the dining room table and were avidly involved in the game.

"What's up?" Harold asked.

"*DragonFyre* just demolished me," she said with a sigh. "I'm out of the game."

Tom's head came up. "How can you be? Your fortress was practically impenetrable."

She shook her head. "I don't know. He's been nowhere in sight for days, then he suddenly appears with all the right questions and all the right answers." She closed her laptop and put her elbows on the table, propping her chin in her hands.

"Is *Comedian2* still playing, even though we know it's not really her?"

Harold was shaking his head. "I haven't seen her, but then I'm working in a different direction. Richard?"

"Hmm?" He continued staring at his screen. "What the hell?"

"What?" Everyone asked at once.

"I just got annihilated."

Megan could see the disbelief on his face. "By who?" she asked.

Only then did he look up. "*DragonFyre.*"

Two of them out of the game in so many minutes? Something was going on. Megan grabbed her phone and called Cal's number.

"What's up?" he asked.

"We don't know, but Richard and I are both out of the game."

"Shit." He mumbled to the side but Megan caught his words. "Someone's on to us."

"Cal, talk to me."

"We're headed that way now. Is Jeff still there?"

"Yeah. He's making up this month's schedule."

"Make sure he leaves you off of it. You're out of the tour business."

"You can't do that. Jeff told me what you figured out, so the danger is in the game, not the tours. Since I'm not in the game anymore, there shouldn't be a problem."

"We don't know that for sure. We're almost there. Just hang on." And he hung up on her.

Megan wondered who *we* referred to. She didn't have long to wait as within minutes the front door opened and Cal walked in, along with three other men Megan hadn't met before.

Cal made the introductions. Harold, Tom and Richard were justifiably in awe that three FBI agents were standing in the living room with them. Megan, on the other hand, was terrified. If the FBI was here, they were in the middle of something well beyond the BPD's ability to handle; something of national proportions.

She looked at Cal. His face was grim but when he saw her look at him, he managed a weak smile.

"Megan, let Agent Morrison have access to your game on your computer," he said.

She shook her head. "I'm out of the game."

"You should still be able to sign on," said Richard. "I'm still watching, even if I can't play."

Megan sat back at the table and booted up her laptop with Agent Morrison standing at her shoulder. "It's not here," she said after a minute.

"Excuse me," Morrison said, practically shoving her out of the chair to take over. His fingers flew across the keyboard, screen after screen popping up, data streams running so fast Megan couldn't begin to decipher what they meant.

"There's an echo, but I can't trace it," he said, getting up. "Let me see where you're at, kid." He walked around to Richard's chair and sat.

Megan watched his eyes as they quickly flickered across the screen as he typed. "Someone is tracking the game and knows exactly where everyone is," he said. "Damn, there it goes." He looked over to where Harold sat. "You still in?"

Harold's eyes got wide. "Yeah." He was already getting up.

Apparently this time, the agent managed to lock something up on Harold's computer. "Got it, bastard," he muttered. He pulled another computer out of his bag and set it up next to Harold's. No one said anything as he silently worked, first on his laptop then on Harold's.

Megan felt she should offer the other agents some coffee or something. Everyone was standing there, watching Agent Morrison work. When Cal caught her gaze, he winked, which made her feel a little better. She went over to stand by him.

Cal called the boys over, made Jeff shut down his computer, and sat everyone on the sofa. He sat on the coffee table facing them.

"You need to know what's going on," he started, then glanced at one of the other agents who had moved to lean against the wall at the end of the couch. The man nodded.

"The men you identified are part of a Brazilian syndicate and are on the FBI's watch list."

"Oh, boy," said Harold. "Like mafia?"

"We won't use that word," said the nearby agent.

"Apparently these men are in the states looking for the Bahia Emerald, which they believe belongs to them, not the various people who have claimed it. The Brazilian's say it was stolen from the mine there and they want it back."

"But we don't have it," Tom said. "None of that's real."

"Remember it's worth over four hundred million dollars. That's very real, and apparently these people won't stop until they locate it. They've somehow found out about the game, realized the emerald is supposedly part of it, and are now after anyone who may have knowledge of it."

"Is that why John Dough got killed?" Tom asked, his voice quivering.

"We can only assume that these men found he was in the game and when he couldn't give them what they wanted, they got rid of him."

"But Lauren was the one who claimed to have the emerald," Harold said. "Why would they kill John?"

Cal shook his head. "We won't know that until we catch the bastards."

Megan took the hands of the two sitting on either side of her, giving them a gentle squeeze. She wasn't sure if her intent was to reassure them, or herself. "So what do we do now?" she asked.

"Sit tight until these guys are caught."

"Does that include me?" Jeff asked. "It sounds callus, I know, but I'm not in the game, haven't been assaulted, and I have a business to run."

Megan could see Cal contemplating Jeff's question.

"Look, it's not like I'm going to tell anyone what's going on," Jeff said. "In fact, I really wish I didn't *know* what's going on."

Cal glanced at the agent next to them, then back at Jeff. "You might want to keep a low profile until we get some closure on this."

"It's August and the height of the tourist season. I can't close up shop."

"God damn it, Jeff. Pay attention here. We're dealing with people who have no compunction about killing if they don't get what they want. If they find out you're associated in any way…"

Jeff put up both hands. "I'll be careful, okay?" He stood. "I've really got to go. Do I need a police escort?"

Cal shook his head in frustration. "Get the hell out of here."

Jeff had only been gone minutes when Morrison hollered from where he had been relentlessly working. "We've got him!"

187

"We've had tech working on this from the get-go," Cal said. "How'd you get in?"

Agent Gardner answered. "We have Morrison."

Everyone crowded around to see, but Harold's computer screen was blank. Morrison's screen, however, was streaming data at an incredible rate.

"Nothing there to see. I'm downloading this maniac's files. As soon as that's done, I'll have control of the game and he'll have nothing. In the meantime, let's find out who this bastard is. The game is registered through a corporation, which is only a shell, but everything is traceable, if you know where to look." As he spoke, he opened another screen and began typing.

Megan saw a quick flash of the FBI logo as Morrison tapped into a secure server and started a search. He turned to face the group. "This person is playing a brutal game, but I have to admit he's a genius. Encrypted within the game software that each player downloads is a GPS file so he knows exactly where each player is anytime they're on line. As game-meister, so to speak, he goes by the name Simon, but he also has an avatar which he can use to delete a player at will."

He glanced back at the screen, which was still filtering data.

"What is his avatar?" Megan asked, although she had a feeling she already knew.

"*DragonFyre*," Morrison said just as his computer pinged.

He looked back at the computer screen. "Our perpetrator lives in New York City. We can have agents at his house within minutes."

Megan saw Agent Norris pull out his phone.

"What's his name?" Cal asked.

"Matthew Langley," Morrison answered.

Megan collapsed in a heap on the floor and Cal grabbed her to try and cushion her fall.

"That fucking bastard," he muttered. "He's not in New York, he's here in Boston," he shouted to Norris, then leaned down to where Megan sat, cross-legged, her head in her hands. "You okay?"

She grabbed his arm. "Stacy." Her eyes were wide and frightened.

"I know." He looked around. All three agents were on their phones, apparently having a system as to who called who because all the conversations were different. Cal had only one call to make.

"Stacy, where are you?"

"Home, of course," she said. "Jeff's here and we have a tour tonight. He says Megan can't do it, but won't tell me why. Is she okay?"

He frantically thought of how he could warn Jeff without him in turn saying anything to Stacy. He decided on another tactic. "Megan's fine, but is having computer problems. Does Matt happen to be there?"

He heard his sister huff. "I haven't seen him in days, and he won't answer his phone or return my texts. I think when he does get around to calling me, I just might not answer mine."

Good for you, Cal thought, then asked, "Do you have his address? Maybe we can drop her computer off at his place."

There was silence on the line. "How odd," she finally said. "I hadn't really thought about it before, but he's always over here or we go out. I've never been to his place."

A strike out for Cal, but a plus as far as he was concerned for Stacy.

"Okay, just tell Jeff to stay close."

"Stay close? What?"

"Just tell him. He'll know."

The minute he got off the phone, he turned to the agents. "Langley's gone to ground. He usually hangs out at my sister's house but she hasn't seen him."

"Your sister?" Agent Norris narrowed his gaze.

"She's not involved. She's only been seeing him for," he paused and it dawned on him. "He started coming

189

around about the time John Dough died and Megan got in the game."

"Oh, god," Megan groaned, looking up from where she still sat on the floor. "He said he was into computer software and it never dawned on me…"

"It's not your fault," Cal told her.

"But there were so many times," she murmured. "It was like he was baiting me, but I wasn't smart enough to understand."

"Baiting?" Gardner echoed.

"Dropping hints; asking me about the game."

"There's no address listed for Langley in Boston, at least not under that name," said Norris. "We'll get APBs out on all four men. In the meantime, we need all of you to stay in one place."

"Can it be at the B&B?" Megan had finally gotten to her feet. Cal put a hand on her shoulder.

"Why?" Norris asked.

"Because I live there and my clothes are there and I need to make sure Stacy's okay."

With each word she spoke, Cal could hear her voice strengthen and he gritted his teeth for the argument he knew was coming.

"Okay," Norris said and Cal looked at him in surprise.

He shrugged. "We need to minimize locations, but there are too many of you to be in one place. Besides, it might look more normal to have her at home. Langley has to know the game is out of his hands now, but he doesn't know who did it. Besides, he already took Megan out of the game, so he must feel she's no longer valuable."

"The boys can stay here," Cal said.

"I'll stay here with Gardner." Agent Norris nodded. "Morrison can go with you and Megan."

Cal took Megan's hand. "Let's go get your stuff." He led her down the hall to his bedroom. The minute he closed the door behind them, he pulled her into his arms.

"I am so sorry, baby," he whispered as he kissed along her hair line. He could feel her tremble. "I should have never let you get in that game."

Her arms wrapped around him, hugging him tightly. She tilted her head back and caught his gaze. "None of this is your fault. I volunteered, remember." Her lips lifted in a wobbly smile. "All for a story."

He kissed away her words, taking her mouth urgently, hotly, wanting to absorb her worry. She answered in kind, her tongue dueling with his, her fists clutching his shirt. What he wouldn't do to go back days, months, and change things.

Reluctantly he released her. "We'd better get back out there."

While Megan picked up her scattered costume, he threw some clothes and toiletries in a bag, knowing he would stay with Megan until this was done.

They came out to find Norris relaxed on the couch, the boys sitting at the table on their computers.

"No game," he said.

"This is an old one," Harold answered. "Agent Morrison checked our computers and they're safe. Besides, we gotta do something."

Gardner was coming out of the kitchen, eating a sandwich. Cal knew there was no reason for it, but he still felt anger well up inside. They were taking over the case, taking over his house, eating his food.

"Stay out of my beer," he said, only to have the agent grin at him.

Morrison rode with him and Megan over to the house. Morrison got a phone call half way there but it must have been unrelated because he didn't relay any information once it ended. Then again, the Feds were known for keeping information to themselves.

Just to make sure, Cal asked, "No news on the APBs?" He watched the man's expression in the rear view mirror. Dark glasses hid his eyes, but his mouth never even twitched.

"We'll keep you in the loop, Garrett."

Damn straight, he thought, throwing the truck in park behind the house. As they walked up to the back porch, he said, "My sister, Stacy, doesn't know anything about

191

what's going on, and I'd prefer to keep it that way if at all possible."

"How are you going to explain me?" the big man asked as Cal stepped up on the porch.

The back door flew open and Stacy appeared. "It's about time. Where have you been, Calvin Garrett? Jeff said Megan was in an accident last night and I've been worried." She stopped in the middle of her tirade when she caught sight of the agent standing just behind Cal. He hadn't realized how tall the man was, but now, a step below Cal, they were eye level.

Morrison wasn't looking at Cal, however, but past him to Stacy. A slow grin spread across his features as he subtly straightened. Stacy had that affect on people.

"Hello, I'm Stacy." She put out her hand. "And you are?"

Morrison's large hands completely engulfed his sister's in a handshake that appeared to go on forever. Cal cocked a brow at Megan but she shook her head slightly, lips curling into a smile.

Cal made a shooing motion with his hands to get his sister to back up. "Can we take this inside? It's hotter than hell out here."

As soon as they entered the kitchen, he made the introductions. "This is Agent Morrison. He's an…associate from another law enforcement agency who's here for a…training session."

His sister would kill him if, or rather when, she found out exactly what he hadn't said.

"Welcome to the Blue Rose Bed & Breakfast, Agent Morrison," Stacy said politely, not tearing her gaze away.

"Call me Tyler."

"Would you like something to drink?" she asked. She glanced over to the breakfast nook where they all usually sat, then back. "Why don't you all go into the sitting room? It's vacant right now, and I'll bring out some drinks and snacks."

Cal didn't know what had gotten into his sister, but it made his gut hurt and he spoke between gritted teeth. "This is fine, Stac. He's not company."

Megan ducked her head but he heard her giggle. His sister shot him an irritated look, and Morrison discretely coughed.

"Sit." He pointed to the bench and the man folded his long limbs under the table, sliding up against the window.

"I'm going downstairs to shower and change," Megan said.

"Now?" Cal asked, with a feeling she was abandoning him.

"Yes." She leaned close to whisper for his ears only. "Play nice."

Cal sat and watched as his sister fluttered around the kitchen making sandwiches. She had always been the ultimate host, he thought, so what was it that irritated him now? He glanced at the agent, whose gaze followed his sister's every movement, the slightest smile curving his lips and crinkling his eyes. His own gaze narrowed.

"So what do we do now?" he asked to draw the agent's attention.

Morrison turned his head and met Cal with a steady gaze. "Now we wait."

Chapter 20

Megan took an extra-long, hot shower, smiling as she thought of Cal upstairs. The sparks had been instantaneous between Stacy and Agent Morrison, although Cal certainly hadn't recognized it. Men.

It might work out well for Stacy since idiot Matt would no longer be in the picture. Then again, she knew the decision was up to Stacy. Just because she was in love didn't mean everyone else had to be.

She dried her hair, pulling it back in a ponytail, then dressed in shorts and a tank top, sliding her feet into comfy flip-flops. She was glad she didn't have to do a tour tonight, although at the same time didn't know what she would do to occupy herself since she was also out of the game.

She grinned, thinking about what she could be doing, with Cal, if not for the three boys at his condo and the FBI watching their every move. She wondered briefly how she could think of making love to Cal with everything that was going on. She could only think that mentally going to that happy place was good therapy in times of stress.

She came upstairs to find Stacy in a dither and Agent Morrison looking helpless as he leaned against the counter.

"Megan." Stacy rushed up and grabbed her hands the minute she saw her. "You've got to help."

"I know. That's why I'm here and not in bed already," she replied. "I thought I'd help with the appetizers for the tour group and as soon as they're gone, I'm crashing. I didn't get much sleep last night."

"No, that's not it. Jeff left to go change and now he can't do the tour," she practically wailed.

Megan's heart pounded as she switched her gaze to Agent Morrison. "What happened to Jeff? You shouldn't have let him leave," she accused.

"Cal told him to go when you went downstairs." The agent shrugged his shoulders. "Besides, he's okay. He just texted Stacy and said a stomach bug hit him when he got back to his place."

"And Tyler said you weren't to leave the house. I don't understand what's going on, and nobody seems to want to tell me." Stacy looked accusingly between the two of them.

"Cal's just trying to protect you; all of us," Megan amended. She looked around the kitchen. "Speaking of, where is he?"

"He got called out on a case," Morrison said.

"I thought *we* were his case," she said.

The agent gave her a half smile. "While every law enforcement officer would certainly like to have only one case at a time, that's just not the case." He grimaced. "No pun intended."

Megan sighed. "Well, I suppose I could do the tour, but remind me to tell Jeff he needs to train more people for this particular tour. It can't continue to be just him and me."

Stacy gave her a hug.

Morrison stepped away from the counter. "You're not going out."

Megan looked at Stacy's crestfallen expression, then back at Morrison. "May I speak to you in the other room?"

He nodded and followed her through the kitchen door to the dining room. Thankfully the tour group hadn't arrived yet.

"You're not going out," he repeated before she could even open her mouth. "Norris would have my head, and Garrett; well, I think he would make my death slow and painful."

She waved aside his concerns. "I'm out of the game and besides, you said Langley didn't have control of it anymore. So either way, I'm not a threat. I don't have the treasure they're after."

195

"Just because you didn't use the emerald as your treasure doesn't mean you might not know where it is, at least to their way of thinking."

"Agent, it's an hour tour, very close to here with lots of people around." She pursed her lips before she uttered what she hoped would be the coup de grace. "Besides, maybe if I did the tour, it would lure them out in the open. I would expect that you would go with me."

"You want to be used as bait?" His tone indicated he questioned her sanity.

She shrugged. "Not really, but I do want this thing to end. If this will help, I'll do it." And she could only hope if there was trouble, her ghostly guardian angel would be there to backup the FBI.

An hour later she was dressed and ready, Stacy none the wiser as to her real reason for doing the tour. One of these days, they really needed to tell Stacy what was going on. She would not see protecting her and keeping her in the dark as the same. For now, she helped set the appetizers on the table and spoke to a few of the tourists anxiously awaiting the tour.

Agent Morrison had said he would check with Agent Norris, and had apparently gotten his go-ahead. When she walked back into the kitchen he was just disconnecting from another call.

"Agent Gardner will meet us at the Charles Street cross-over," he said. "The kids are secure in the condo and Norris said he could handle things there. I'll feel better with two of us in an uncontrolled, open environment." He then made a face.

"What else?" Her stomach already had butterflies.

"That whiz-kid, Harold, wanted to come with Gardner. He said something about a ghost."

Megan had to smile at the big man's discomfort. "You don't believe in ghosts, do you, Agent?"

He hesitated before shaking his head. "I believe in what I can see, like evidence, not speculation."

"You sound just like Cal. Did they teach you that in police school?" She smiled to take the sting out of her words.

He returned her grin.

"Now, get rid of the tie and suit jacket," she said. "You don't exactly look like a tourist."

He loosened and removed his tie. "This stays on," he said as he grabbed the lapel of his coat, pulling it open to reveal his shoulder holster and gun.

* * *

The group tonight consisted of another family reunion, this one more than thirty strong. Whenever Megan wasn't narrating, the youngsters asked questions, which she happily answered when she could. If she didn't know, she said so, and mentioned several books available from local bookstores.

Morrison stuck to her like glue, never more than a step away, even when the children crowded around her. When they got to the cross-over, she remembered to caution him that her candle lantern would be covered as the re-enactors by the oak tree did their parts. He nodded, saying he would wait at the top of the ramp where he could see in every direction until Gardner caught up with them. She led the group down the circular ramp to the grassy Esplanade.

"It is said of this night that the young patriots' arguments for forcing the British to leave their beloved Boston were quite adamant, and that Logan Mallory's voice rose loud and clear above the rest." Megan set her candle lantern down on the ground and covered it with the black cloth just as the re-enactors' lanterns were lit. Everyone's attention was focused toward the river as they began their portion of the story.

"What are you doing here?" A voice hissed in her ear just as she straightened back up. "You're not safe."

She spun around and directly into Matt, except it was a battered and bruised face glaring back at her. He reached out to grab her arm and she jerked away, stepping back.

197

Her foot kicked the candle lantern, and she heard glass shatter.

Frantically she looked around for Agent Morrison, but the area where they stood was completely dark; the only light that of the re-enactors' lanterns twenty yards from where she stood.

"Fire!"

Megan turned to where her candle lantern, breaking when it tipped over, had started the cloth on fire. She lifted her skirts to try and stomp out the small flame. The tourists were scattering, paying no attention to the play still going on down the hill by the oak tree.

"I'll get it," Agent Morrison said, pushing her aside to stomp on the cloth and the grass around it.

Megan stepped back, speaking softly to get the crowd back in focus. All eyes turned again to the play just as Toni's scream came from the oak tree. No one noticed that Megan screamed, too, as an arm circled her waist, dragging her backward into the dark. A scream that was cut short when her mouth was covered with an evil smelling rag.

* * *

Cal was drag-ass tired by the time he finished the paperwork on this latest case. The scumbag he'd been tracking for months had finally been caught trying to rob a convenience store. Wanted for several felonies, Cal had had to show up for booking. There ensued an argument with the guy's public defender, who had demanded bail, of all things. With a sigh, he tried to clear it from his mind as he pulled up behind the Bed & Breakfast. He wished he was going to see just Megan. Instead, he had to contend with an FBI agent, his sister and whatever was going on with her.

The back door was locked, which was unusual unless everyone was gone. He put his key in the lock as he realized – everyone should *not* be gone. He shoved the door open and quickly walked through the inside porch to the kitchen.

It took a minute to untangle the scene that met him. Agent Morrison, jacket off and black smudged shirt half untucked from his trousers, was bent over a chair, tying someone's hands together. Cal stepped to the side and realized it was Langley, face beaten with a cut still seeping at his mouth and one eye swollen shut.

Agent Gardner stood close by, gun in hand.

"Where are Stacy and Megan?" Cal's first thought was the girls' safety.

"I sent Stacy downstairs out of the way," Morrison said, straightening. He gave a slight grin. "She wanted to punch him, but someone had already done some damage."

"Megan?" Cal's question was met with silence.

"Where the hell is Megan?" He stepped closer to Gardner.

"We don't know." The agent hesitated, raising his gun just a little higher.

It didn't scare Cal. He slammed both hands against the agent's shoulders, knocking him back against the wall. Curling one hand into a fist, he reared back to smash it into Gardner's face, but Morrison caught his arm. Cal tried to shrug him off, but the giant was stronger.

"It was my fault," Morrison said. He slowly released Cal's arm. "If you want to hit someone, hit me." He narrowed his gaze as he straightened, a full head above Cal. "But you only get one."

Cal's shoulders slumped. It didn't seem fair to hit a willing opponent.

"Look, we're handling it," Morrison said, his tone placating.

"And just how the fuck are you doing that?" Cal ran his hands through his hair. "How did he get in here and take Megan and still be here?" He jerked his head towards Langley.

"I din't take 'er," Langley tried to speak around his cut lip. Cal thought he might have a tooth or two missing, too. "I was tryin' ta warn 'er."

"Shut the hell up," Morrison told Langley. "You've spouted lies from the get go."

Cal took a closer look at Langley. Someone had beaten the shit out of him and the man looked scared. He glanced down at Morrison's hands, then over to Gardner.

"No, we didn't beat information out of him," Morrison said, reading Cal's thoughts. "He was that way when we collared him at the river."

"At the...what were you doing there?" he asked before it dawned on him. "Don't tell me you let Megan do a tour?" Cal felt his palms itch. "You tell me that and I'm going to kill you, outside where your blood won't mess up my sister's kitchen."

Gardner looked like he believed Cal, but Morrison smirked, knowing it was a bluff. Instead, he gave Cal what the man knew he wanted.

"We called your captain and Agent Norris and they have men out looking for Megan. We thought we would see what this scumbag knows."

"I've got to find Megan." Cal started for the door, only to have Gardner step in front of him.

"Find out what he knows first." He nodded toward Langley.

"That will take about thirty seconds," Cal growled, stomping over to where Langley cowed in the chair. He put up his tied hands, swatting his ears and waving across the front of his face.

"I'm not going to hit you, although I really, really want to."

"It's not; there's something here," he said in agitation.

"You've got thirty seconds to tell me what you did with Megan."

"Didn't take 'er," the man said again.

"Who did?"

Cal saw fear flash across his face before he reached up to rub his right ear, then his left.

"I don't like repeating myself."

"They want the emerald. They thought I had it 'cause someone put it into the game, but I don't. So now they're going after other players." He practically wailed.

"Is that why John Dough was killed?"

Langley rapidly shook his head. "I don't know. I didn't kill anyone." Again he swatted at something only he seemed to see.

"But you gave them access to the game so they could locate everyone with the GPS device. You had them targeting Megan, you asshole." Cal stood, closing his hands into fists, using all his control not to bust the guy in the face.

"They threatened to kill me if I didn't help them. When I found out they were targeting her I took her out of the game. I took those boys out, too. I tried to close the game by taking out all the players, but something happened on line."

He was madly waving the air in front of his face. "When they found out today that I can't control the game anymore, they beat me up and said there were other ways to get what they wanted."

"What other ways?" Morrison asked. "Jesus Christ, stop twitching."

Langley practically fell out of the chair with his wiggling; his bound hands waving wildly.

Cal grabbed Langley by the shoulders and shook him. "Where is Megan?"

"I don't know," he cried. "I tried to warn her, down by the river. But there was a fire and it was dark and then I got hit from behind."

Cal looked up at Morrison for verification.

"Long story short." He nodded. "I stomped the fire out, but in that time, he was on the ground and Megan was snatched."

"Why the hell was she doing a tour anyway?" Cal frowned. "I told Jeff to take her off the schedule."

"Jeff texted and said he had a stomach bug at the last minute." Morrison shrugged.

Cal paced to the counter and back. Jeff never got sick. Just that morning he had been adamant about continuing the tours and had said he wouldn't put Megan on again until this was over. Cal pulled his phone out and called. When it went to voice mail, he texted, using the code he and Jeff had developed during college. It was their way of keeping in touch, and no matter what they were doing or where they were, they answered the text the minute it came in to let the other know he was alright.

Can't talk. Sick.

He stared at the message on the screen. Not the right answer.

"Jeff didn't send that text. Someone's using his phone, which probably means he's been taken, too."

Again, he stood in front of Langley. "Where were they taken? Where did they beat you up?"

"I don't know where they went. They caught me outside the hotel." His hands were again waving in front of his face. "God, get these bugs off me."

Cal stilled. He stepped away from Langley and watched the man, first looking intently and then glancing to the side hoping to see something out of his peripheral vision.

"Do either of you see anything buzzing around Langley?" An idea was beginning to form – a totally far-fetched, insane idea for finding Megan.

Both the agents shook their heads. "Is anything buzzing around you?" He asked the agents a second question but still stared at Langley.

"No," they both replied.

Cal took his phone again, scrolling through the contacts for the one he needed – Keith Farrington.

Chapter 21

Megan slowly surfaced from some deep, very dark and cold place. She didn't move at first, trying to orient herself and figure out what exactly had happened. Her right shoulder hurt, as though she had been hit hard. As her senses became more alert she realized she was lying on that shoulder, apparently on concrete. She could feel its cool, grainy texture beneath her cheek.

She opened her eyes but nothing changed. Wherever she was, there were no lights, no windows, no cracks beneath the doors; if there were doors. Even as her eyes adjusted, the air only went from black to deepest gray. She listened for anything that might indicate where she was. When she heard a sound, she sucked in a breath and held it, then realized it wasn't a person coming closer, but the sound of waves. Another breath confirmed it as the tangy sea salt air filled her lungs.

She automatically reached for her phone in her pocket and realized two things. One was that she had on her historic costume so there were no pockets. The other, most importantly, was that her hands were tied behind her back.

That brought her to a third realization. She was not here by accident. She had been taken. What she had thought was a dream came back to her in a flash – the tour, the fire, seeing Matthew Langley.

"Damn you, Jeffery Garrett," she muttered as she wiggled around trying to get upright, which was made doubly hard as her feet were also tied together.

"I was thinking the same thing," came a voice from behind her, "although I really think it should fall on Matthew Langley."

She screamed, squirming in the opposite direction.

"Megan, stop. You're giving me an even bigger headache."

She had sucked in a breath to scream again when his words caused her to pause. She recognized that voice.

"Jeff!" She was at once relieved to have him close by, and panicked. "Untie me. We have to get out of here."

"There's just one small problem." She heard a thud, like a heavy footed hop, then another and another. "Keep talking," he said.

"About what?" she asked. "Maybe about how I'm going to punch you for getting sick so I would do the tour and be out in the open?"

"I wasn't sick." *Thud, thud.* "Some goon caught me outside my apartment and knocked me out."

Thud, thud. Megan felt a foot at the small of her back. "Don't hop again; you'll stomp me."

She heard, then felt, Jeff sit down beside her. She managed to roll over, bumping up against his thigh.

She felt immensely better knowing she wasn't alone, even tied up, in a dark, damp warehouse.

"I'm sorry you got caught up in this," Megan said, struggling to sit up.

Jeff snorted. "Yeah, so am I." There was a pause then he added, "I didn't mean it when I said this morning that I wasn't concerned. That all I cared about was my business."

Megan sighed. "I know. Somehow your entire family has gotten wrapped up in this horror, all because of a fake treasure." She wiggled around until she felt she was facing Jeff. "Right now, we have to figure a way to get out of here. I doubt anyone knows where we are, so no one is going to save us except us."

She used the heels of her feet to pivot on her fanny. Her hands, behind her, slid along Jeff's thigh toward his butt.

"Hey." He started to wiggle away.

"Just be still. We might be able to untie each other if I can get to your backside."

"Megan, it won't work."

"Sure it will. They do it all the time in the movies." She scooted along the concrete floor towards his back. She clumsily felt along one arm to his wrist. Her fingers, practically numb, fumbled before finding his binding. She then realized why he had said it wouldn't work. Whoever had taken them had used zip ties.

She was just about to ask if Jeff had a pocket knife tucked away when a door creaked open at the far end of the building. Megan took a breath, prepared to scream for help. But what light appeared in the doorway illuminated a massive body; much larger than Cal or the FBI agents.

As he entered the room and closed the door behind him, fear took over.

"Sh," Jeff said when she whimpered. "Don't let them know you're scared."

"Like I can help it."

"There you go…get mad."

For several long minutes, she heard nothing but silence; no footsteps, no breathing; nothing.

"Keep your back to mine," Jeff whispered when at last they heard movement.

The steps echoed through the cavernous room and it was hard to tell just how far away the man was. Megan was sure there was only one, and it probably would have been easy to overpower him had they not been tied.

Suddenly a bright light shone right in her eyes. She blinked and squinted, unable to see past it to whoever held it, but she recognized the voice when he spoke.

"You will give us the treasure now." The gruff demand had her pushing her back against Jeff's.

"I told you before, there is no treasure. It's all a game; a prank." Her voice shook slightly as she spoke, all the while her brain looking for a way out of their predicament.

"It is no game. It was stolen from our government." The voice was closer, but Megan still couldn't see who was behind the light. "If you do not tell, I will have to hurt your friend here."

Jeff was abruptly pulled away from her back. "Hey," was all he got out before Megan heard a fist slam into flesh.

"He hurts easy." The light wavered and Megan caught a brief glimpse of Jeff lying unconscious on the concert floor, blood oozing from his mouth. The man bent toward him again.

"Wait. No. No more. Please." She frantically tried to think up a plausible location for the imaginary emerald but the buzzing in her ears was making her dizzy. She tucked her knees up and put her head on them, trying to think. The buzzing increased and she realized it wasn't nausea. She looked toward the light, which she knew the man held, and could just make out a green haze.

A green haze.

"Laurie, you have to help us," she whispered. The green haze surrounded the man, making the light waver as he tried to shrug it off.

"Get it off!" The man growled, circling almost as fast as Laurie was spinning, causing the light to look like a strobe. "Get it off, or I will kill your friend."

Megan couldn't see a gun, but regardless, knew the man was large enough not to need a weapon.

"Laurie, go find Cal. He can save us." She only hoped the ghost had as much faith in Cal as she did. After all, it had taken a lot of convincing for Cal to even believe there was a ghost. How on earth was Laurie supposed to make him believe she could help?

The green haze disappeared and for a moment Megan felt herself relax. But as the light, and the man behind it came closer, she wondered if Cal would get to them in time.

* * *

Cal pressed the intercom button on the wall by the kitchen door. "Staci, come up here." He then turned and paced impatiently across to the window and back, checking his watch and wondering how long it would take Dr. Farrington to get here. When he had said he would send a patrol car, the professor said it would be quicker to grab the red line.

206

"Cal, what's happening? Where's Megan?" His sister flew into his arms and he hugged her tight.

Just as quickly she stepped away and headed straight for Langley, kicking him viciously in the shins.

"Where is she?" Stacy accented each word with another blow from the toe of her shoe.

"Ow! Make her stop!" Matt tried to move aside, but Stacy was quicker.

"I don't see anything," Morrison said. "Do you?"

Cal and Gardner shook their heads, although Cal did put his hand on Stacy's arm.

"Stac. I need to ask you something." He looked at Langley who was back to twitching. What he was about to ask would put his professional position as a detective on the line, but there was no way around it.

In a low voice, he asked, "Do you see her?"

Her brows furrowed. "Who; Megan? No, I don't know—"

Cal shook his head. "Laurie," he said in a whisper. His sister's eyes widened before she whipped back around, searching the kitchen.

"No, I..." She paused as she stared just beyond Langley's shoulder. "I don't. Megan seems to be the only one who sees her."

Morrison's brows arched and Cal thought -- *here it comes*. But the agent didn't say anything; just pinched his lips together.

"Laurie, are you here?" Stacy asked. "Please..." her voice trailed off as the front door bell rang. "Who could that be?" She turned and started for the front hall but Cal stopped her.

"I'll get it." Cal hurried out of the kitchen and through the dining room and sitting room.

"Hello," he said pulling open the front door to admit Dr. Farrington. "Thanks for coming on such short notice."

"Not at all," he replied. "I would do anything to help Megan, as she's given me some first rate research." He patted the small, square black box that hung around his neck, as he followed Cal back to the kitchen.

The instant the professor entered the room the box started squawking. "Oh, my," he said, his voice in awe.

"So you think she is here?" Cal asked.

"I can't see her, but the electromagnetic energy is very strong." The box made a higher pitched sound the closer the professor got to Langley.

"Who exactly are we supposed to be seeing?" Gardner asked skeptically.

"A ghost," Cal stated simply.

Gardner snorted. "Right."

The professor's little black box quit beeping. He turned this way and that but only silence filled the big kitchen.

"God damnit, Gardner," said Cal, "shut the hell up."

Gardner straightened from where he had been lounging against the wall. "You have no right to talk—"

"Shut up, Mitch," Morrison told his partner, a frown on his face. "If Garrett says there's a ghost, there is a ghost."

Cal shot Morrison a look of gratitude before he pulled up a chair in front of Langley, straddling it, with his arms casually draped across the back. He didn't look at Langley, but instead focused on the area behind him. He took a deep breath and blew it out, briefly closing his eyes. He had to get the words right; had to make her understand how important this was.

"Laurie, I hope you're still here because I need your help. I know a long time ago, you and your true love, Logan, were unjustly separated and your love was irrevocably lost. I know you're still here because you are looking, trying to find what you lost so long ago."

A soft *beep, beep,* came from the professor's machine.

Cal wished he were alone in the room. As a guy, he just didn't go around exposing himself like he was about to do. But it couldn't be helped.

"I think you know what I need. Like you, I've lost someone I love more than life itself; ripped away from me just as you were taken from Logan."

The machine beeped faster and louder, the only sound in the room other than Cal's voice.

"Some bad men have her, and I believe with all my heart that you can help me find her. I know Logan felt he failed you all those years ago when he couldn't find you. Don't let me fail Megan."

The machine fell silent for an instant, but when the professor turned slightly, it began beeping again.

"Oh my stars," whispered Stacy. "I do see her. She's by the back door."

All heads turned in that direction. Gardner reached for his gun as Morrison stepped closer to Stacy. Apparently Stacy could see the physical manifestation of Laurie. Cal didn't see anything. He had to take all this totally on faith and his belief in, and love for Megan. He stood, reaching out a hand.

"Please help me."

The professor's machine went ballistic. The lights blinked rapidly, the beeping becoming a high pitched shriek, increasing closer to Cal.

"She's gone," Stacy said. "I don't see her."

"No," the professor replied. "She seems to go into a frenzy, moving too fast, when something excites or provokes her. When I recorded her at the park that first time, Megan didn't see *her*, but saw a green haze around the man who was trying to hurt her. Yet down at the wharf, she said she saw the young woman. A spirit can present itself in various ways. It could be that Stacy can see her shape but not see the green haze, whereas Megan has seen both. Perhaps this frenzy mode is her way of telling us something."

The professor tried to follow the sound, turning again toward the door. "I pick up the energy only when this is pointed directly at her," he said, indicating the black box. "I believe she's back at the door."

"She wants us to follow her," Cal said.

"This is fucking bullshit," Gardner said. Cal tossed him a look as he headed toward the door. The man's face was pale, a nervous twitch in one eye.

"I'm going," Cal said.

"Wait for me." The professor said, followed closely by Stacy.

Morrison took a step toward the door then turned and looked from Langley to his partner. "You don't want in on the action; fine. You can stay here and guard the prisoner. But hey, this is going to be a hell of a lot more interesting."

Cal stopped in the back yard. "Stacy?" The thing about siblings is you know what the other wants with just a word.

"I don't see her, Cal," she said. "I don't think I'll see her in the dark."

"Professor?" He could hear the soft beep-beep of the little black box.

"As long as I can keep her in front of me, we can walk as fast as she wants to go." The machine beeped faster and the professor headed through the parking lot to the street.

"Walk?" Morrison asked.

"How else are we going to follow her?"

Cal grabbed Stacy's hand and hurried after the professor.

They kept up a lively pace west on Charles Street and across Revere. The machine quit beeping and Cal thought the professor lost her at the corner of Pinckney. It took a few minutes with the professor pacing back and forth, before the signal again flared.

After several blocks, Cal looked up and took in more of his surroundings, whereas he had been concentrating only on the constant sound of the black box. "We're heading for the harbor," he said as they stopped at Somerset in Government Center.

"That might make sense," Stacy said, "since Laurie's father had warehouses at the harbor."

"Wait." Cal stopped the group in the middle of the sidewalk, halfway down the block.

He looked around, knowing he wouldn't see Laurie but hoping she would know he was looking. "Laurie, I know Logan worked for your father at the warehouse, but we're looking for Megan. Please take us to Megan."

The professor's box squawked and squealed and Cal felt a tingle around his head just before something struck him between the shoulder blades, propelling him forward. He grabbed a nearby park bench to keep from falling.

"I don't think she likes that you implied she didn't know what she was doing." Morrison actually chuckled.

"Okay, okay," Cal muttered.

The professor lost the signal again at School and Washington when they turned right. Backtracking to the corner, they found her again at Court, which turned into State Street.

"She's quite the GPS," Morrison said, the signal growing stronger the faster they walked toward the harbor.

Cal was on his phone calling for backup at the wharf. He didn't know how many they were up against but figured at least three, as that was the number of different men they had encountered so far. Cal wanted better odds.

It was late enough that there weren't many tourists near the wharf. The tour trolleys had quit for the night. As soon as a patrol car arrived, he instructed the officers to block off Long Wharf and to send more uniforms down the wharf after them as soon as they arrived.

"Hold up, professor," he said when the man kept walking, close to the building but further away from the protection of the group.

"The signal has changed," he said, holding up the box. The series of lights were flashing, as though in code, and the beep had become a long, steady sound like the flat line on a heart monitor. The professor stood in front of a padlocked door. There was no insignia to indicate who it belonged to, and it was on a section of wharf without street lights.

The others gathered closer. Cal saw another patrol car pull up and waved the officers over.

"Cal, I see her," Stacy whispered with a tug on his sleeve.

Just as she spoke, the black box went completely silent.

"She went through the door," Stacy exclaimed.

Cal and Morrison pulled their guns, as did the patrol officers. "Professor, you and Stacy get back over here." He indicated the area behind him.

"But—"

"Now!" He grabbed his sister's arm and pushed her behind him.

"We're going to have to shoot the lock off," Morrison said after examining the device. "Keep everyone back. I should be able to hit it at an angle where the bullet will deflect that way." He pointed to the garden area across the sidewalk.

Cal glanced at the officers, then Morrison. "On three."

Chapter 22

Megan frantically scooted across the concrete floor, away from the ever approaching light and the man behind it. She wanted away from Jeff, hoping after hearing him groan that he was conscious and could somehow do something.

A shot rang out and she screamed, curling into a ball and waiting for the pain she knew would follow. Instead, there were shouts, more gunfire and a heavy weight fell across her legs, pinning her down.

She screamed again, twisting and turning, trying to get loose. Someone grabbed her from behind and she fought frantically, sobbing Cal's name, knowing she would never see him again to tell him she loved him.

"Baby. I've got you." A hand caressed her hair. "Sh. It's alright now."

She sucked in a breath and smelled Cal, his unique scent coursing through her veins and calming her. Her bindings were cut, and numbly she turned, burying her face in his chest, murmuring "I love you" over and over again.

She heard the rumbles in his chest, unable to distinguish words, finally giving in to the fear that had held her captive.

* * *

"You should have taken her to the hospital," a disembodied voice floated across her consciousness.

"Fuck that. I can't let go of her." Pressure increased across Megan's shoulders, but she didn't fight it, knowing this was something good, something right.

Warm breath caressed her forehead; a hand rubbed her arm, nudging her to consciousness.

"Cal?" She forced the word past her dry, scratchy throat.

"Right here." Warm, firm lips kissed her temple.

Images flashed across her mind; horrible sounds as she and Jeff fought for their lives.

She jerked, her eyes popping open.

"Jeff!" She struggled to sit up but Cal held her fast.

"Jeff's fine, Megan. Everyone's fine." This time his words were firm, although there was an underlying tenderness.

She finally looked around her, realizing she was no longer in a dark, cold warehouse but instead in the kitchen at the Bed & Breakfast. Stacy stood there crying, with Agent Morrison's arm around her shoulders. Jeff stood close to her on the other side, a bag of frozen peas held against his jaw. She sat on Cal's lap near the breakfast nook.

She tried to reach for the glass of water on the table, but her arms felt leaden. Cal anticipated her need, tipping the glass to her lips until she pulled back.

She looked again at Jeff and Stacy, faces she held dear, but when she turned to Cal, she burst into sobs. "Oh, god. God," she managed to moan. "You saved us."

She felt more than heard the rumble of a laugh in his chest. "Well, I have to admit I had some help."

"Where? How?" She didn't know where to begin her questions.

"Later, sweetheart. You need to rest." Cal started to stand with her in his arms but she turned, throwing him off balance enough that he sat back down.

"No. I'm...fine," she hesitated, and then realized that she actually was. Other than a few bruises, she felt better than she had in days, knowing that the threat was over.

The back door burst open, spilling Tom, Dick and Harry into the kitchen, followed by Agent Norris. Everyone started talking at once. Megan smiled as Jeff stretched his arms wide, exaggerating the size of their attacker. She snuggled back against Cal's unrelenting embrace until Agent Morrison gave a piercing whistle, effectively shutting down the noise.

"How can anyone hear anything?" he questioned, which only served to start everyone talking again, giving their description of the occurrences or asking more questions.

"Please?" Megan said softly and it was more effective than Morrison's whistle. Everyone stopped and looked at her. "What really happened?"

Cal put up a hand when Jeff started to speak. Jeff shrugged and leaned back against the counter.

"We found you and Jeff in the warehouse. The bad guy with you, Vincent Silva, easily gave up the location of the other two, thinking they had diplomatic immunity. Even though the Brazilian government wants them for questioning regarding the emerald, they have waived their rights because of the murder here."

Cal looked over at the boys. "You'll be happy to know the L. A. police have located Lauren Harding. She was stashed in a cabin up in the mountains with a body guard. They apparently hoped to use her as collateral for the emerald."

Megan saw Harold grin.

"As for Langley," Cal continued, "he's facing all sorts of accessory charges but I imagine he'll get some kind of plea bargain. Either way, we won't be seeing him again."

He looked directly at Stacy. "The next time you decide—" His words were interrupted by Megan's elbow in his ribs.

"But what about Laurie?" Harry questioned. "I talked to Professor Farrington and he said Cal asked her to help. Has anyone seen her since?"

The room fell silent. Megan looked at Cal, who gave an embarrassed shrug. She smiled tenderly at him knowing he had opened his heart completely for her.

"Maybe she did what she was here to do and knows we don't need her anymore so she has moved on," Megan said softly, knowing her words were inadequate but how could any of them know what a ghost thought?

* * *

The first weekend in October was gorgeous. The leaves were changing, painting the landscape in an array of color that reflected off the clear blue of the water. A warm breeze wafted across the surface, gently pushing the sailboat toward the outer islands. With only one sail hoisted, it drifted hither and yon, in no particular hurry to get anywhere special, because its occupants were already exactly where they wanted to be – together, and alone.

"We could have brought Tom, Dick and Harry," she said.

"All on planes home," he replied, placing a kiss to her brow.

"What about Stacy and Agent Morrison?"

He frowned. "I haven't decided if I like him yet."

She laughed and turned to straddle his lap. He was tempted to lash the tiller so he could get both hands on her luscious body, but contented himself to look…for now.

"How about—"

"How about if you tell me again what you told me at the warehouse?" He tugged her close with one arm, nuzzling between her breasts, most of which were exposed above her skimpy top.

She looked demurely down at him. "That you saved us?"

He slowly shook his head.

Instead of answering, she wound her arms around his neck, leaned close, and set her lips on his. Her kiss started slow and tender, and he tried to remain passive, just to see what she would do. But patience was beyond him.

The kiss escalated with explosive heat, and he realized there was no hope for him.

"Hold that thought," he choked out, setting her aside to quickly drop the sail and the anchor. As soon as he felt the anchor catch he grabbed her hand and tugged her down the few steps to below deck.

They were quickly rolling across the bed, arms and legs entwined, heated kisses consuming them.

"Tell me," he groaned succumbing to the temptation of her breasts as he buried his face in their lushness.

She squirmed beneath him. "What?" She continued to tease, tickling his ears with her fingers.

"You're killing me." He captured her hands and held them against the bed. His gaze captured hers and he watched as her expression turned serious.

"She came back because of you and me. She needed to make sure we found each other."

"What?" He stilled. That was not what he had wanted to hear.

"Laurie. She only showed up again when I returned to the *Castle* after being gone years. She needed to know that hers and Logan's love wasn't in vain. That their kind of love would endure through us." She looked up at him with solemn eyes.

"And will it?"

She wrapped her arms around him. "If you love me as much as I love you, how can it not last forever?"

"Forever and then some," he whispered, bending to tenderly kiss her.

The End

If you loved this book
(or even just liked it)

Please leave a review ...
Authors need reviews! Keep this author writing.

Barbara Baldwin books also published by Books We Love

Lost Knight of Arabia
Spinning Through Time
Prospecting for Love

Barbara loves to travel and explore new places, which usually means each of her novels is set in a different locale. She has been published in formats from poetry and short stories to full-length fiction, but she really loves writing romance, whether it be contemporary, historical or time travel. Just for fun, each year she writes a Christmas short story for family and friends—some heartfelt and others whimsical — but always a gift from her heart. She has an MA in Communication, has taught at the college level and has made over 100 presentations at state and national conferences. She also loves to create art through pottery and fused glass, candles, baskets and quilts. Visit her website at http://www.authorsden.com/barbarajbaldwin.